RETRIBUTION

INDIGO RIVER
PUBLISHING

RETRIBUTION

A T.K. WALLS *NOVEL*

Indigo River Publishing
3 West Garden Street, Suite 718
Pensacola, FL 32502
www.indigoriverpublishing.com

Editors: Dianna Graveman, Regina Cornell
Cover & Book Design: mycustombookcover.com

Ordering Information:
Quantity sales: Special discounts are available on quantity purchases by corporations, associations, and others. For details, contact the publisher at the address above.

Orders by US trade bookstores and wholesalers: Please contact the publisher at the address above.

Printed in the United States of America

Library of Congress Control Number: 2019946972

ISBN: 978-1-950906-10-9

First Edition

With Indigo River Publishing, you can always expect great books, strong voices, and meaningful messages. Most importantly, you'll always find . . . words worth reading.

Contents

One

EMILY LEFT HER OFFICE EARLY TO WALK ON THE BEACH. She didn't care that the usual clear blue sky was gradually growing darker or that the wind was rapidly picking up. After leaving her hectic life, a broken relationship, and a job in Boston to move to a quiet seaside village, she had grown fond of the breeze and the sound of the waves gently crashing onto the beach. She had spent a grueling day in negotiations with an uncooperative client, and she was looking forward to a brisk, relaxing walk along the shore.

The access nearest the beach was practically empty; she quickly parked and was on the sand in moments. The sky was darkening, and the wind was becoming stronger, forcibly blowing the sand across the beach. The sand felt like thousands of tiny needles striking her legs. Regardless, the walk was what she needed. The smell of the water, the sound of the crashing waves, the touch of the wind against her skin, and the feel of the cold mist upon her face helped slowly ease the effects of the stressful day on her body with every step.

There he was, lying face down, his blond hair glistening in what remained of the sunlight, the surf gently pushing him farther up the beach. He was wearing a black wet suit with a dull red stripe running down the left side. At first glance she thought he might have been swimming, but it soon became obvious he was probably dead.

She froze, staring at him, not able to walk any farther. He looked familiar, but then again, he didn't. Catching her breath, she slowly inhaled and called out to him. When he didn't respond, her fear that he was dead became a reality. She should have walked away and called the police, but instead, mesmerized by the surf gently pushing him back and forth onto the sand, she slowly walked to the body. She found it odd—in an almost funny, grotesque way—how his head remained motionless on the sand while his body gently went up and down with the surf. Still looking at him and without thinking, she took her phone from her pocket and called 9-1-1.

Police and rescue workers took what seemed an eternity to arrive on the beach. Meanwhile, onlookers gathered and gawked. The tide was coming in, yet no one touched the body, not even to pull him farther onto the sand. Once the police arrived, the typical yellow crime-scene tape sectioned off the area where the body had floated onto the beach. The rescue team pulled him out of the water and turned him over. His once-glistening blond hair was now matted with wet sand; the skin on his face was smooth and yet somewhat bloated. Again, Emily felt there was something about him that was almost familiar. But then it was gone. She tried to look away but found herself glued to the scene unfolding in front of her.

"Excuse me. Are you the lady who called in the body?"

Emily's eyes were frozen on the body, and she didn't hear the police officer speaking to her.

"Excuse me, lady," the officer said again, louder this time. "Did you call nine one one to report a body?"

Emily jumped at his voice and turned to look at him when she realized he was speaking to her. "Uh, yeah," she stammered. "I saw him while I was walking. I thought he was swimming ashore. I didn't realize at first he was dead. Who did you say you were again?"

She was now acutely aware that he might not even be a police officer. He wasn't wearing a uniform or police jacket, and he wasn't wearing any visible identification. In fact, she would not have guessed he was a cop. His hair was longer than she expected, and he was very tan. He wore khaki shorts with a black "Las Vegas" sweatshirt, and he was barefoot. If he was a cop, she wasn't impressed.

"I'm Sheriff McNeil. You can call me Mac. I need to ask you a few questions and get some basic information. Your name and address to start with, and any other information you may have such as what you saw before you approached the victim. What beach access did you use to come onto the beach? Did you notice anyone leaving the parking area or the beach?"

"How about one question at a time, Sheriff?" Emily asked. Even though she could easily remember his questions, she wasn't about to answer them in rapid-fire fashion. If he expected answers from her, he needed to slow down, ask her one question at a time, and allow her the courtesy of answering before firing off another question.

"My apologies," he replied curtly. "Let's start this again. I need your name and address."

"I'm Emily Bridges, and I live at seventy-four nineteen Hartford Street."

"Hello, Emily. Did you park at the beach? If so, where is your car parked?" Sheriff McNeil carefully watched Emily while she spoke. *She seems overly confident and calm for someone who just found a dead body on a beach*, he thought.

Emily explained where she had parked and that she didn't see anyone or anything on the beach until she saw the body. What she didn't tell the sheriff was that she was so lost in her own thoughts she could have easily passed someone on the beach without noticing, and she certainly didn't tell him that instead of immediately calling the police when she saw the body, she walked closer to the body to check him out. As she answered his questions, she noticed that Sheriff McNeil was not writing down her responses. He stood listening with his hands in his pockets. He did not interrupt her but allowed her to freely speak.

When she was finished, he resumed his questions. "Emily, where do you work?"

"I have a new law practice on Monroe Street in town," she responded softly. "Well, I didn't actually open a new practice; I took over Russell White's practice when he retired. I guess you can say I inherited his clients." Emily stumbled over her answer, not sure why she was nervous. She was never nervous—not in court, not in her personal life, and never after seeing a dead body, and she had seen several of all ages. And most certainly never when talking to law enforcement. None of these things made her nervous or anxious. With years of experience as a prosecuting attorney, she often went to the site of a reported death. She wondered why this one was bothering her.

The sheriff looked her over. She looked like a lawyer. She was wearing a black suit jacket with white trim, a light-blue blouse, a skirt, and no shoes. Her pale legs were bare. The only piece of jewelry she was wearing was a clunky, odd-shaped gold bracelet. Given the time of year, she didn't look like a local, either: no tan. He knew Russell had sold his practice, but he somehow missed whom he had sold it to. "Emily, how long have you lived here?"

"I just moved here a few weeks ago. I bought the blue house near the cliffs. You can almost see it from here. Why?" Now she was paying attention to his questions.

"I'm just asking questions, Emily. You're new in town, walking on the beach, maybe for the first time, and you stumble over a body in the surf that doesn't appear to be from the area. Now that's an interesting welcome to our little town, don't you think? I mean, what are the odds? Are you certain you don't know him?" He waited for her to speak, intently watching for a reaction.

Emily found herself getting angry. "How do you know he isn't from the area, Sheriff? Do you know who he is? And, no, I do not know him. Do you think I put him here and then called you? Or better yet, do you think someone else put him here in the hopes I might go for a walk and find him?"

Mac studied her face, her expression and demeanor. If she was lying, she was damn good at it. Something about the scene didn't ring true to him. With over twenty years' experience as a police officer and having worked the majority of his career in homicide in Boston, he knew a staged scene when he saw one. He was willing to bet this guy didn't drown, and he doubted he died in the ocean or on the beach. He was also willing to bet Emily knew exactly who he was. She may not have recognized the sheriff, but he recognized her.

"I'm done for now. If I need anything else, I'll give your office a call," he said as he turned away from her and walked back toward the coroner's wagon.

"That's OK," Emily called after him. "I am easy to reach if you need anything more, either at my office or through my paralegal."

Instead of turning around to acknowledge he had heard her, he raised his hand and kept walking. She found it rude and unprofessional, but brushed if off as arrogance and simply poor manners.

The growing crowd of onlookers stayed even as the body was loaded into the coroner's wagon. Sheriff McNeil was amazed at how seemingly normal people would gawk at a dead body. He scanned the crowd looking for anyone who didn't belong, anyone who seemed out of place. It was hard to imagine that any of the locals would be involved in this guy's death, but he knew from his many years in the business that anyone could be a killer. He took several quick photos of the scene, including the crowd, the body, and Emily. He remained at the scene until the body was loaded into the coroner's wagon. Before leaving, he took one last sweeping look at the area where the body was found. Seeing nothing of importance, he got into his car and followed the wagon to the morgue.

Two

Seth worked every day Monday through Friday. He went to work at the same time every day and parked in the same spot each day. The only variation to his rigid routine was his office hours. The office receptionist was an older woman who was just as rigid as he was. She kept the office spotless and managed the office with ease. When he left after work, he went to the same store to buy a few fresh things for his dinner. His home routine was just as rigid as his work routine. His refrigerator was basically empty. He liked it that way. Empty was cleaner. He never ate leftovers.

He was very strict with his routine. He kept his yard clean, grass neatly mowed, and shrubs trimmed. He was never late for work, and he paid every bill before the due date. Even his mortgage and association fees were paid in advance. He had discovered as a child the quickest way to avoid questions, prying neighbors, and unannounced visitors was to always pay bills early. Even in college, he managed to budget what little money he had to pay the bills and have enough left over to eat.

His home was just as well kept as his office, but not spotless by any means. He didn't like clutter, but he did like his living space to appear "lived in," and he was meticulous about keeping his floors clean. On his walls were scenic pictures of places he had visited or of places he wanted to see.

There was only one picture that wasn't scenic; it was taken during a time in his childhood that he never wanted to forget. The frame looked as if it had been made by a child, and it was. The photo was placed in the foyer on top of a narrow entryway table. He kept fresh flowers and a seasonal candle on the table next to the picture. It looked almost like an altar, but it wasn't. He just wanted to see the photo whenever he came home and whenever he left. He needed to see the photo. The photo made him happy, even if it was only for a brief moment. He couldn't look at the picture without feeling a twinge of chest pain, and when he did, he couldn't breathe. He knew some day the ache—that pain—would go away, and he dreaded the day it did. The pain kept him going and gave him purpose. He longed to feel the pain and the inability to breathe, even if it was for a moment. He stared at the picture, and when he could breathe again, he slipped off his shoes and walked into his living room.

The living room walls were painted a light green, with dark-green curtains covering the windows. When he purchased the house, he had the carpets replaced with an off-white short-pile carpet. The carpets were the same color in each room. His furniture was simple but comfortable: a large, overstuffed beige couch with a purple blanket folded and neatly placed over the back, and a matching recliner. He had one end table between the couch and the recliner, but no coffee table.

He turned on the TV before sitting down. Channel 6 reported on the late news that a male body without identification had been found in the surf. The reporters were already speculating that the guy was not a local. Their assumption was based on the fact that no one recognized him and that he didn't have a tan; most of the locals spent a lot of time outdoors.

Seth watched the news, interested but not excited by the attention the body was getting. He enjoyed the speculation of how the body ended up on the beach, how the person had died, and who he was. Seth had carefully removed anything that would identify him. Even if the police discovered the floater's identity—and they would—they wouldn't connect Seth to the body. He had never been questioned about bodies randomly discovered. In the early years, killing was simply something he did, perhaps even for practice. But now he hadn't killed in years and had truly thought he would never kill again. But certain events had led to his decision to start again down this path, and the guy on the beach was part of a bigger plan. His death was just a start. There would be more bodies.

The news reporters were no longer interested in sensationalizing the floater's fate once they realized the crowd at the beach was thinning. Seth listened to the Channel 6 reporter give his opinion of who the floater was, where he came from, and how he turned up on their beach at the end of a busy work day. Nothing the reporter said had any basis in fact. He was just like all the other reporters on TV. They gave their opinions without knowing the facts and expected people to believe them. Each reporter was trying to get his fifteen minutes of fame. When the news showed the body being loaded into a coroner's wagon, Seth turned off the TV.

Three

The body was sent to the local county coroner's office. Sheriff McNeil knew the coroner would be out, as it was after regular hours, and either a medical student or a resident would be performing the intake. Leaving nothing to chance, McNeil accompanied the body to the morgue. He wanted to make sure whoever was doing the intake treated the body like a crime scene, which it was. Samples for evidence would need to be gathered from the body, and pictures would need to be taken. He would rather see too much being done than enter a courtroom with not enough evidence to convict. He also wanted to make sure nothing got contaminated. Having solid evidence thrown out of court due to contamination was far worse than not having enough to convict.

The morgue was in the same building as the county health department. The entrance for the morgue was at the rear of the building. The coroner's wagon pulled alongside the rear doors of the morgue. The driver rang the intercom buzzer.

"Yeah?" came the almost immediate response.

"We have a body that needs dropped off. Hey, the sheriff is with us! He said he needs samples for evidence. Can you open the loading dock door?"

Without a response, Mark, the night attendant who doubled as the coroner's intern, threw open the doors and secured them. "Hi, Sheriff. You guys need any help unloading?"

"Good to see you, Mark," said McNeil. "I can't tell you how glad I am that you're on tonight. This one will need to be processed for evidence, and we don't have an ID yet. Is your boss here or out of town?"

"Dr. Davis just left for the weekend. I think he was going out of town; he didn't say. You want me to call him, Sheriff?" asked Mark.

"Sure, you may want to give him a heads-up. Just in case he wants to come back for this."

Mac and the coroner knew each other well, and Mac knew his friend might be upset about getting a call on his way out of town, but he also had no doubt Dr. Davis would come back to the morgue.

...

Duval County was the smallest county in New Hampshire, and the coroner's office was staffed with only one pathologist, Dr. Ryan Davis, who ran the medical examiner's office and performed scheduled autopsies during the day. The county kept a couple of medical students on board who covered the morgue intake during night shifts and holidays.

Dr. Davis started working as the county coroner right out of residency. He couldn't imagine a better job: no being on call, no complaining patients or families, and he always had holidays and weekends off. Not to mention he earned about the same as his colleagues. He had been brilliant in his studies but lacked the social skills necessary to practice medicine at the bedside. He craved his freedom, and working long hours plus taking call was simply something he refused to do. He was selfish with his time and preferred to keep contact with patients to a minimum. He enjoyed working eight-hour days with nights, weekends, and holidays off, and he liked the solitude of his job. His position as chief medical examiner for the smallest county in New Hampshire assured him a lot of flexibility and a comfortable lifestyle, and gave him the freedom he needed.

Dr. Davis was attractive, or at least he thought so. He was an easy six feet tall, with dark hair, blue eyes, nice teeth, and an average weight. He took pride in his appearance and religiously worked out whenever he could.

He had recently canceled his engagement to Sherry, his girlfriend of seven years. She was also a physician, and over the years, they had spent less and less time together. Their relationship had become more of an exercise in excuses not to see one another than taking time to be with one another. Even talking on the phone had become a chore, and most of their communication was via text message. When he suggested they cancel their engagement, she seemed relieved—almost happy. The conversation came easily, and they chatted more than they had in months. He thought he should feel sad, depressed, or at least a little unhappy, but instead he felt relief. He was looking forward to no more forced conversations or making text excuses to cancel plans, or making plans he had no intention of keeping. And he knew she felt the same. They parted as friends, or at least they said they did.

After his breakup, he had planned a nice, long, quiet week alone. He was looking forward to fishing and hiking, and simply being alone with his thoughts and his dog, an aging shepherd mix named Max. The dog was well trained and usually very quiet. If Max barked, Ryan knew there was a problem. The dog was close to eleven years old, and Ryan had adopted him from a rescue when he was two. In the nine years he had had Max, he could count on one hand the number of times he had barked.

Ryan was driving out of town to his cabin with Max lying next to him on the seat, snoring as he slept. They had just left the county when the deputy coroner called to ask for assistance with a body found at the beach.

According to Mark, the sheriff had requested he call him back. He had recently employed the medical student as his intern to cover the morgue when he was out of town. The morgue was rarely busy, but someone had to be available for intakes. Medical students and residents made great employees. Most needed the money, and they were usually accountable and excellent with records. The intakes that required an autopsy were usually from car accidents or unexpected deaths from one of the local hospitals. Occasionally autopsies were arranged by families who suspected medical malpractice. Regardless, all of these were managed Monday through Friday, during normal business hours. Autopsies were not performed on the weekends. Mark could easily handle natural-cause deaths, or even deaths the local police suspected resulted from other than natural causes, such as a suspected homicide. He knew how to collect samples for evidence. But when Mark called, Ryan could tell something was different about this body and this autopsy.

"Hey, I am really sorry I have to bother you, Dr. Davis." Mark's voice was shaking with excitement. "The sheriff asked me to call you. He said you might want to come back. They found this guy floating on Hampton Beach. He didn't have any identification, so I logged him in as a John Doe. He was wearing a wet suit, and at first, I thought he had probably drowned. However, his lungs are dry—I mean they don't have any water in them! I already ran his labs, and so far nothing is unusual or abnormal. I think you should come back to do the autopsy. I don't think this one can wait a week. The sheriff has already been here, but he isn't here right now."

Mark was in his final year of medical school, waiting to find out where he would be going for his residency. Even at the sheriff's request, he wouldn't have suggested the pathologist leave his vacation on a whim. He paused, waiting for Ryan to answer. He suspected Ryan wouldn't be happy to come back, if he came back at all.

Ryan let out an audible sigh. "OK, Mark, I'll come back. There had better be something to this John Doe, and he'd better not be a heart attack guy who died while scuba diving! Oh, and tell the sheriff—who I know is standing next to you—that he owes me for this one!" Ryan tried to sound irritated, but he gave it away when he laughed.

"Yeah, yeah, he's right here." Mark continued talking excitedly. "Dr. Davis, seriously you have to see this guy. I don't think he died at the beach or anywhere near the beach. This is going to sound crazy, but I think the wet suit was put on him after he died. In fact, I think this guy has been dead for a few days. The body is moderately swollen, but the wet suit isn't stretched. If he died in the wet suit, the suit would have naturally stretched as the body bloated. But this wet suit is too large for the body, even with the bloating. Hell, it's even too long for the guy! John Doe is about five feet, eight inches, and this suit is made for a much taller guy!"

Ryan was now intently listening. Without even thinking, he had turned the car around and was driving back to the city.

Max raised his sleepy head to look out the window as Ryan did a fast U-turn, and then looked back at Ryan. Patting the dog on the head, Ryan said, "Not today, big guy. We will go another time. The lake house isn't going anywhere."

He hadn't worked on a homicide or an interesting autopsy in years. He was bored with autopsies to determine if a physician or hospital was responsible for some elderly person's death. Mark's description had his mind racing, and despite his desire to leave town, his need to get out of town, this body spiked his curiosity, not to mention there was only one coastline in New Hampshire, and Hampton Beach was very small. He also knew that Mac would not have suggested his assistant call him if this one wasn't going to be an interesting one. And truth be told, he was intrigued, and he couldn't wait to get back to the morgue.

Dr. Ryan Davis arrived at the morgue and quickly changed

into scrubs. Mark had the body on the metal slab and the wet suit on a table next to the body. One glance and Ryan understood why Mark was excited. Even with the body bloating, the wet suit was obviously too large for this guy. But that wasn't what was alarming. In the center of the guy's chest were what looked like two characters branded into his skin: *J* followed by another *J* or the number 1.

Ryan pointed to the guy's chest and asked Mark, "What the hell is this, and where is the sheriff?"

"Dr. Davis, first, the sheriff had to leave, told me to tell you he would be back in the morning, but you can call him if you need him." Taking a deep breath, Mark continued, "OK, second, when I saw those marks, I knew the sheriff and you should see this as soon as possible. I think someone killed this guy! How else would those marks get there? It looks postmortem to me."

Ryan quietly examined the tissue surrounding the branded characters. He didn't respond to Mark. He wanted to examine the body in silence. Using a flashlight, he closely examined the body. When he was done with the preliminary check, he motioned for Mark to come back over to the table. "Mark, did you get photos of the chest? We need a close-up of those marks too."

Mark nodded his head in understanding. "Yes, I took photos of the marks and several more of the body, and I logged them into evidence as required. I noted the marks were probably postmortem. He was wet, even with the wet suit on. He had some type of oil or lotion on his skin. I took samples of that too. I think whatever the substance is, it was used to make it easier to get the suit on this guy."

"Well, the body isn't wet now. Did it dry, or did you clean it off?" Ryan checked the skin folds, looking for the substance Mark had found on the body.

"I think maybe being exposed to air dried it, but I did get samples." Not wanting to miss anything the coroner did, Mark stood opposite Ryan and intently watched as he completed his exam.

"That's OK if your sample wasn't enough. The skin samples

ought to indicate what the substance was, even if it dried on the body." Ryan completed his examination of the skin folds and looked over at his assistant. "Hey, I am glad you called me. After a very quick preliminary exam of this poor guy, I agree with your observation that he didn't drown. He was obviously placed in the wet suit after he died. Maybe oil or some other lubricant was used to help get him into the suit. Did you notice that the bloating of the body is not uniform? I would think the areas where the suit compressed the skin are where the bloating is less, and the areas that were looser are where the bloating is greater. Did you take photos of the body in the suit? Before you removed the suit?"

"Yes, I did, Dr. Davis. I already downloaded the photos to the computer." Mark showed Ryan the photos that were taken of the body before the suit was removed.

"Mark, notice on the pictures where the suit is bunched up on certain parts of the body that don't bend, like between the elbow and shoulder? Now look over at the body. Those areas where the suit would have bunched up are not uniformly bloated with the rest of the limbs. The tightness of the suit prevented the bloat. You're correct: it looks like the suit was placed on the body after he died and probably after rigor set in too. No way did this guy put on that suit."

Ryan found himself excited to actually perform an autopsy that wasn't a routine confirmation-of-death autopsy. "OK, Mark, great job. Let's get started with this autopsy. Go ahead and turn on the recorder."

Ryan formally began the examination of the body. He turned it over to examine the back and the sides. He felt the back of the head and found what appeared to be the cause of death: a single gunshot wound entering the back of the skull. But as Ryan examined the entry site, he noticed the site lacked bleeding, the edges were well approximated, and the entry wound was small. "This guy was also shot postmortem, probably a small-caliber bullet," he said. "We'll get that out later."

He then performed the standard Y cut, and removed and weighed the organs. Nothing was unusual with the internal organs. He took sections of the liver for later analysis, along with blood and other tissue samples, including a sample of the tissue around the branded characters. So far nothing indicated a cause of death. The last organ to examine was the brain. After removing the top of the skull, Ryan removed the brain, weighed it, and again took sections for analysis. He quickly located and removed a .22-caliber bullet, but it was obviously a postmortem wound.

"Mark, from all appearances, this guy was seemingly healthy. Let's get a look at the wet suit. When you examined the suit, did anything appear unusual besides the lubricant?"

Mark cleared his throat, looked at the suit, and replied, "I only removed it and took pictures of it. I didn't examine the whole suit. I did take samples of the substance, though." He had been so engrossed in the body that the last thing he was thinking about was the wet suit.

Ryan slowly began to examine the suit, starting with the zipper. He pulled the suit inside out to ensure every part of the interior was examined. "Mark, can you get the black light? I think there is something on the inner aspect of the back of the suit."

Mark brought the black light to Ryan, who slowly shone the light on the back of the suit as he started to examine the material. Ryan then took samples of a jelly-like substance that he was certain was a type of lubricant used to stuff the suit on the deceased. When he was finished, he removed his gloves and looked at the slab. *What did this guy do to end up getting stuffed in a wet suit and dumped on a beach?* he wondered.

Four

Mac headed home after leaving the morgue without waiting for Ryan to get there. He knew Ryan would spend all night at the morgue and call him in the morning if he found anything. It was already late, and Mac also knew if he went back to the station, he wouldn't leave until the next night.

Having never married, Mac lived alone, but he still put his service weapon in a lockbox that sat on top of his desk in his home office. He sat behind his desk and began the task of making a file for the John Doe found at the beach. He didn't need the autopsy report to tell him this guy had been murdered. After twenty years working for the Boston Police Department, mostly as an investigator in the homicide division, he knew a crime scene when he saw one.

Mac had left Boston at the ripe old age of forty-one, after he was recruited to work temporarily as an interim sheriff for this little seaside community of Reagan, New Hampshire. Reagan was just west of Boston, close enough to go to Fenway and yet far enough to get away from the hustle and congestion of the city. And it had a nice little beach. After his tenure as interim sheriff, he entered the election race for the office and easily won. That was almost ten years ago.

The crime rate was relatively low in Reagan. The crimes that kept Mac the busiest were complaints of barking or howling dogs at night, loud music, missing bikes, or the occasional adolescent shoplifter. The county hadn't seen a murder in at least sixteen years. Mac had a staff of four full-time officers and six part-time officers. They covered the entire county, which included four small towns with a total population of about twenty-six thousand.

The body floating along the shore was the most excitement the sheriff's office had seen in years. Even though Mac had hopes the guy had just drowned or had a heart attack or something, he knew in his gut the results of the autopsy would show something else. He wasn't sure how the community would handle a murder investigation. He wasn't even sure if his officers knew how to manage an investigation.

...

Morning came too quickly for Mac, and along with it, a backache. He stumbled into his kitchen rubbing the small of his back with his right hand, and with his left hand he turned on the coffee pot. Still walking hunched over, he ambled into his bathroom hoping a hot shower would lessen the muscle pain. The shower and coffee woke him up, and soon he was back in his car heading to the station.

He was sitting at his desk when he heard his dispatcher take a call from the coroner.

"Good morning. Reagan Police Department."

"This is Ryan Davis. I need to speak immediately to Sheriff McNeil," Ryan said to the dispatch operator.

The police dispatcher was an older woman who had been at her post for as long as Ryan could remember. She put him on hold and walked into the sheriff's office.

"The coroner is on the phone for you; says he needs to talk to you immediately."

"Thanks, Van." Mac picked up the phone. "Sheriff here. What's up?"

As soon as Ryan started to speak, he realized he was talking a bit too fast and sounding a little too excited for an experienced pathologist. He had no doubt his friend would call him on his excitement, and knowing the call was being recorded, he cleared his throat and made an effort to sound like the medical professional he was.

"Sheriff! Uh, Mac! I just finished the preliminary exam on the body found at the beach. There are a few things you need to see. I could go over this by phone, but I think you need to see this for yourself. Plus, I am not sure how secure your office is. I don't want anything leaked to the press. How soon can you get down to the medical examiner's office?"

"On my way," Mac answered quickly. He was already standing when he hung up the phone. He shouted his destination to Van and practically ran out the door to his car.

The ME's office was adjacent to the local hospital and just a few blocks down the street from the city-county building, which was where the sheriff's office was housed. Mac arrived at the office within minutes. Ryan was waiting for him at the entrance to the building and handed him gloves and a mask. The medical examiner and sheriff had known each other for several years and often worked together on cases. Outside of work they were friends and occasionally went deepwater fishing together along with a group of other locals, but at work, they were business all the way. If a case ever went to court, neither wanted their findings challenged based on their friendship or unprofessional behavior.

"Good morning, Sheriff. I'm glad you came. We were up all night with your John Doe." Smirking, Ryan continued, "I'm certain you were aware that I was on my way out of town when my assistant, Mark, called me in. He told me you thought I should get started on this one rather than wait a few days. Good thing you thought to call me in."

"Uh, yeah, look, I am sorry about that. We both know that cabin isn't going anywhere!" Mac said lightheartedly. "Besides, I knew you would want to see this one. You and Max can head up there once this is all over."

"I may just do that and keep my phone off this time! Seriously now, Sheriff, we noticed a few unusual issues with your John Doe. Let me show you this guy."

Ryan led Mac into the exam room. After numerous years as a police officer and having seen dozens of autopsies, Mac was more familiar with the process than he cared to think about. He still thought of the morgue as one of the coldest and most unfeeling, sterile places someone could work. It amazed him how easily Ryan chatted while performing an autopsy and how his friend even managed to drink coffee in the same room as the body. With this autopsy, both Ryan and Mark seemed excited, curious, and eager to explain the details of their findings.

"First, the markings or letters in this guy's chest, if you will, were made postmortem. The markings appear to be the letters *JJ*." Ryan pointed to the John Doe's chest. "Not only are there what appear to be branded or burnt marks on his chest, they were applied after he died. There is also a small bullet wound to the back of the head. This also occurred after he died and is not the cause of death." Ryan paused for effect before going over to the table where the wet suit was displayed. "Now, when we examined the wet suit, we noticed something even more unusual. I thought you would be interested in this." Ryan gestured for Mac to follow him to the table where the wet suit was laid out. "Mark will show you the residue that is remaining on the wet suit. The same substance was also found on various parts of this guy's body."

Using a penlight, Mark illuminated the residue and pointed out the location of the substance that coated various areas of the wet suit.

"So, you think this substance, whatever it is, is unique?" Mac asked while peering at the suit.

"We won't know until we get the results back from the crime lab," Ryan answered. "Find the chemical composition of the substance, and if it's unique, it could help us identify where he was killed. And that could lead to not only who this this guy is but maybe even his killer."

"Whoa there, Ryan, until you have a cause of death, all we have is a dead guy in a wet suit found floating on the beach. There is no evidence he was murdered. You just said the bullet wound is postmortem."

"Mac, if you will notice, where the residue or substance touched the wet suit, it caused a discoloration of the suit material. Both my intern and I suspect the residue is petroleum based," Ryan explained.

Nodding his head in understanding, Mac replied, "The branded letters—that's more than unusual. It doesn't make any sense. You haven't identified him? Has anyone come forward to say they are missing a family member, a husband, a brother, anyone? If I understand you correctly, you don't have a cause of death, he was shot and marked up after he was dead, and that wet suit is completely in one piece. No bullet holes? Any tears?" Mac realized this was not going to be an easy drowning or even an easy murder. Lowering his voice, he asked Ryan and Mark, "You don't have any idea how he died, do you?"

Ryan shook his head. "No, I have no idea right now. I just sent off the samples to the lab. Once we have those back, I may be able to give you a cause of death. But at the moment, I have no idea. What I can tell you after my preliminary exam, Sheriff, is the victim is between the ages of thirty-five and forty-five, with no indication of heart, liver, or renal disease. No prior fractures and no blunt-force trauma. I also sent out a toxicology screen. Maybe that will shed some light on the cause of death."

The sheriff was intent on keeping the meeting professional. "Dr. Davis, Mark, this autopsy can't be made public. We can't have the public thinking there is a maniac on the loose, killing people and branding them with letters, stuffing them in wet suits and then dumping them on the beach! The only information about this autopsy that can be disclosed is the cause of death. I don't even want the bullet wound disclosed. Do you both understand?"

"Sheriff, you are not dealing with idiots!" Ryan said, visibly angry. "I am fully aware of what can be disclosed and how to disclose the results of an autopsy during an investigation! I called you down here not to get a lecture on how to perform my responsibilities and duties, but to inform you of the current state of affairs with this body! If you remember, you called me back from my vacation to examine this guy. And by the way, finding reports on missing persons is the job of your department, not mine. In fact, my job is to identify the body once you provide missing-person information to my office. Hell, right now, all I can tell you is that this guy did not die in the surf, he did not drown, and he certainly didn't die yesterday. And he didn't put on that wet suit! Someone put it on him, and some sort of lubricant was used to get it on him. He died at least three days ago. His internal organs had signs of exposure to very low temperatures, not freezing but very cold. The decomposition on this guy isn't what should appear after three days, but it should be. It only appears to be hours, at the most maybe twenty-four. This means he died, someone had the means and ability to keep the body cold, and then this poor bastard was placed in a wet suit and dumped on our beach."

Ryan paused for effect, but the sheriff didn't respond. "And when I do find out the cause of death—and trust me, Mac, I will—and when I determine as close as possible the time of death and the manner of death, you, Sheriff, not the media, will be the first to know!"

"Of course. I apologize," said Mac. "I wasn't inferring you didn't know how to do your job. Or that you would run to the media. I am just ensuring we handle this accordingly and properly so that when we do find the guy responsible, we don't risk losing a conviction. This county hasn't seen a murder in over sixteen years. None of our county prosecutors have ever prosecuted a murder case."

Mac could feel his face turning red. The last thing he wanted was for Ryan to think he wasn't capable of managing this investigation, or that he had somehow forgotten how to do an investigation. It may have been ten years since he left Boston PD, and at least that many years since his last homicide, but he hadn't forgotten how to do an investigation. This town was supposed to be his retirement community.

"Look, Ryan, I know you know what you are doing, and you know I am more than capable of working with you on this case as well as managing the investigation. Let's work together on this one like we have worked on other cases. The only difference with this one is that this guy isn't a suicide and he didn't die of natural causes. I think we are in agreement that we have a lot more going on with this guy than just his death. We need to figure out as soon as possible who he is. Perhaps once we know that, we can figure out who killed him and why. I have a feeling that if we don't find out who he is soon, something else is going to happen."

"OK, Mac," said Ryan. "As you know, the lab tests will take a couple of weeks. At the very least, maybe someone will report him missing and we can identify him. Otherwise, we wait and say nothing."

Five

SETH HAD NEVER LIKED THE HOUSE. It was a large, looming, ominous-looking piece of architecture that sat at the top of a hillside cliff in the middle of a town much too small for a house of its size. The house could be seen from almost anywhere in town. In its time, it signified wealth and success. It was built out of imported light-red bricks from England at the height of the natural-gas boom. The bricks had been painted over the years until it was no longer the beautiful, rich, rustic red color but a pale, dingy yellow. The monster of a house contained servant quarters complete with two kitchens, one for the family and another for the factory workers. Adjacent to the workers' kitchen was a large rectangular dining room designed to feed the employees. The house was built next to a glass factory his family had owned. His grandfather had built the factory and the house, as well as the surrounding smaller homes for their workers.

The house also contained a library, two master bedroom suites with sitting rooms, five additional bedrooms, seven fireplaces, and a grand ballroom on the third floor. The staircases were massive and elegant and made from imported wood from the Black Forest, with large floor-to-ceiling windows at each staircase landing. The house during its prime was the jewel of the town. Today it sat in decay and rot, its history and grandeur long forgotten. Seth had inherited this house from his father, who had inherited it from his father. He had grown up in this house. Over the years the house had fallen into disrepair, and the cost to maintain it was extraordinary.

Built in the early 1900s in northern Massachusetts, the house had once been a lovely modern home for his grandfather's family, but it was also designed to support at least a hundred factory employees. In the case of bad weather, the employees utilized an underground tunnel that led from the house to the factory. In keeping with the times and his grandfather's vision of the future, the tunnel had steel doors and various places for lighting. After hours his grandfather would lock the doors leading to the house.

Over time, industry left the area and moved to larger cities, leaving the factory behind. The small rural town could not compete with rapidly growing cities, and eventually the town also fell into disrepair. When the factory closed in the 1960s, his father sealed the doors leading from his house to the underground tunnel, and the smaller homes around the factory were sold. The last surviving reminder of more affluent times was his grandfather's house.

When the house and the factory were first built, they used steam from a pond for heat. The pond was located at the bottom of the massive hill upon which the house sat. At the bottom of the hill and just past the pond was a large ravine. A small pump house sitting next to the pond supplied steam to both the house and the factory. Over the years, the factory had been dismantled until all that remained were the exterior walls. But the pump house was left fully intact. Only the pipes leading from the pond into the pump house were disconnected.

The rest remained. Perhaps it had been too difficult to dismantle, as it was at the bottom of the hill next to the pond, or maybe it had simply been forgotten.

Seth now owned the property that was once his grandfather's, and he had hired a property management group several years back to look after the factory, house, and grounds. Even the property group had forgotten the pump house, which was probably a blessing in disguise, as his second kill was lodged in the large pipes that remained in the pump house.

His first kill had happened purely by accident. As a young adolescent, he had discovered how to open the sealed doors to the tunnel that ran from the house to the factory, and was showing the tunnel to his classmate. The boy's name was Tim. He was a year younger, slight in size, and initially eager to see the long-forgotten tunnel. But after Seth opened the doors, Tim became scared and tried to run from the basement. Desperate to show his friend the tunnel, Seth grabbed Tim and dragged him toward the heavy steel doors, losing his grip and allowing the steel door to slam shut on the child. Tim was killed instantly.

At first, Seth was scared. He was afraid to move, afraid to say Tim's name. Blood was pouring from the other boy's head; his eyes were open and staring at nothing. When Seth realized Tim was dead, instead of going for help, he sat in the tunnel for what seemed like hours, talking to the lifeless child. He knew he had to hide the boy. He couldn't keep playing with the corpse. Eventually the body would smell and his parents would discover his secret. He carried Tim through the tunnel toward the factory and set him up against the entrance door. Before he left the tunnel, he cleaned up the blood. His parents never went into the basement, and no one knew he had been able to open the tunnel doors. But he wasn't taking any chances that someone would go into the basement and see the blood.

As the years went by and he grew into an adult, Seth continued to visit Tim whenever he checked on the house. Even as the body decomposed and eventually became only bones inside tattered clothes, Tim still looked the same to Seth as he did the day he had first come to play.

Thinking of his early days made Seth smile. Tim was not only an accident; he was also an awakening. It had surprised Seth that Tim's death didn't bother him. Yes, he was scared at first. He often wondered why he'd been scared, because Tim's death had actually excited him—so much so that he was curious to discover whether his excitement would grow if the next time he killed intentionally.

He had been twelve when Tim died, and he was still twelve when he committed his second killing. But this time, the killing wasn't an accident.

The second kill was also a playmate, but someone he had never played with before. The homes originally built for the factory workers had now become low-income rental homes, and unattended children were abundant. One particular child usually wandered the streets and often made his way to the pond.

Seth spent the afternoons watching the child from the window of his bedroom on the second floor of the house. His bedroom was in one of the old suites that had a turret window. He stood in the turret watching the boy make his way down the hill to the pond, a plan developing in his mind as to how he would kill him and where he would hide the body. He quickly decided the perfect hiding place would be the empty pipes that remained inside the pump house.

One afternoon in late fall, he noticed the boy was alone, skipping rocks into the pond. It was quickly becoming dark as Seth made his way down the hill. Within minutes, he was along the shore of the pond. He gathered several small, flat, round rocks and started to throw them across the water, making them skip. Soon he and the other boy were skipping rocks together.

"Do you want to check out that old shack?" Seth pointed to the pump house along the banks of the pond.

"What for?" asked the boy.

"Maybe we could make it into a clubhouse or something," Seth said, easily convincing the child to go into the pump house. Once they were inside, Seth removed a thin steel pipe from the liner of his coat and struck the boy alongside his right temple. The child instantly crumpled to the ground. Seth waited to see if the child would move. He didn't feel scared. What he did feel was excitement, a rush. He liked that feeling. He didn't feel the need or desire to talk to this child; there was no reason to. He didn't even know his name. Instead he placed the lifeless body inside the pipes, pushing him in as far as he would go. After he was done, he threw the steel pipe he had used to strike the child into the center of the pond. Then he sat down by the water's edge and waited until the sun was completely down before making his way back up the hill to the house. Once back in his room, he kept watch over the pump house

...

These days he usually checked on the property a couple of times a year. He ensured the grounds were well maintained and not an eyesore. To keep the bodies from eventually being found, he tried to make certain the county would have no reason to enter either the house or the pump house.

Seth walked up the front steps to the house, unlocked the large wooden doors, and stepped into the foyer. Closing his eyes, he took a deep breath. When he opened them, he imagined the house as it had been during his childhood. Instead of seeing dust, dirt, and large empty rooms, he saw the library with books on every shelf, and the dining room table with perfect place settings. If he listened closely, he could hear his mother humming in the kitchen.

He walked through the downstairs, looking into each room, and then made his way upstairs. His first stop was his bedroom. He opened the door and walked immediately to the turret window and looked down at the pump house. It was the same as it had always been, with the exception of being surrounded by weeds and scrub trees. Unlike with Tim, Seth never returned to the pump house to visit the other boy. He had always been satisfied with just looking down at it from his window.

There had been others during his youth, of course, years ago. The playmates had been an awakening of sorts. He never felt remorse or guilt over his kills, and he never had a need or desire to keep souvenirs from them. He had always been careful to make certain he wasn't connected to them, and oftentimes he wasn't even aware of their names.

As he turned to leave his room, he thought about the body he had left on the beach. This time there was a loose connection, and he hoped the police wouldn't be smart enough to piece it together before he finished with his plans. After his plans were completed, he truly didn't care if he was finally connected to a kill, but not before. In fact, he didn't care what happened to the house, the factory, or even the pump house once his mission was complete.

He took one last look at the house, checking to ensure it was safely secured. Before leaving he doubled-checked the basement. Satisfied that the house was locked and his secrets still safe, he closed the massive wooden front doors and walked down the half-moon-shaped concert steps to the sidewalk. Before getting into his car he looked over at the bungalow home that sat to the right of his house.

Six

Boston was good to Dr. Bradley Rivers. Brad, as his friends and family called him, lived a life of privilege. He had wealthy parents and had always attended exclusive private schools. He had grown up with the finer things in life and craving more. His parents gave him everything he wanted and denied him nothing. When it came time for college, Brad insisted on attending a local state university. His parents balked, but in the end he got what he wanted, as usual. What his parents later discovered was that Brad's desire to attend the state university had more to do with his high school sweetheart, Rachel, than with academics.

Brad and Rachel had met when they were both cast in their high school play, *Barefoot in the Park*. Rachel played Corie Bratter, and Brad played the part of her husband, Paul. The play centered on the newly married couple and their adjustment to living together in New York City. Brad was instantly in awe of Rachel. She was a strawberry blonde with small curls that framed her face. When she spoke, the corners of her mouth turned up slightly, and she was most beautiful when she smiled. Brad knew when he met her they would someday marry.

The couple did get married the summer after graduation and before they each went to Harvard, he as a medical student and she as a law student. They rented a small apartment near Harvard Square and struggled through graduate school, living on ramen noodles, eggs, and grilled cheese sandwiches. Rachel completed her law degree but never sat for the bar exam, instead focusing on Brad's career and starting their family.

Rachel loved to promote her husband, and helping him build his practice was her passion. They decided to wait until after Brad's residency to begin having children. The oldest two were boys, and the younger two were twin girls. Rachel and Brad were active in their children's school functions and activities, and they attended church every Sunday. By all appearances, the family led a perfect life.

Brad had built a nice medical practice, specializing in facial plastic surgery. His specialty was reconstructive surgery for accident and burn victims. He spent several years building his practice and enjoyed being at the top of his field. In the early days Rachel was his office manager and was responsible for hiring the staff, who adored her. Every year she hosted a dinner party for both the staff and partners.

During his free time, which was limited, Brad learned to fly and earned his commercial pilot's license. Soon after earning his license, he bought into Krannert, a small independent airport located in Reagan, New Hampshire. It was there he met his future business partner and lawyer, after Eric redeemed his gift certificate for flight lessons. The two men quickly became friends and colleagues, and eventually Brad put Eric on retainer as legal counsel for the airport as well as for his medical practice. Both men had a passion for flying and an equal passion for money. Eric also earned his commercial pilot's license, and the two close friends opened their own exclusive international charter service.

Brad took his family on frequent trips by private plane from Krannert to their winter home in Palm Beach, Florida, with occasional shopping trips to New York and Chicago. He enjoyed flying so much that when he wasn't working in his medical practice, he was in the air. Brad made it a point to always be cheerful, kind, and compassionate. At least that was how his friends described him. However, the nurses he worked with would describe a different person altogether. The nurses found him rude, intolerant, and lacking in compassion, which was in direct contradiction to his specialty.

Rachel planned the family's annual holiday shopping trips. She loved the trips—the shopping, the restaurants, and the time alone with her husband. Brad always picked the location, as he usually combined a little business for the airport with the trips. Between Brad's work and his passion for flying, Rachel rarely saw him. But she had learned that to love him meant she had to share him with these things. She busied herself with fundraisers to help finance the airfield and keep it open, as well as numerous other charity events in their Boston community. Their children attended private schools, but they were also involved in local events and charity functions

...

Rachel's usual morning routine involved getting the kids ready for school and getting Brad his breakfast, a task she looked forward to since this was the only time during the busy day she'd have alone with him to talk.

"Honey, what do you want this morning for breakfast?" she said as he entered the kitchen. "I have eggs and bacon, but I can also make oatmeal or pancakes. Coffee is already poured for you, and I added your cream. Just the way you like it!"

Brad put his arm around her waist and pulled her toward him, kissing her lightly on the cheek. "Whatever is easy for you to make. I am sure I will like it. So, what have you planned for the Rivers family annual shopping trip?"

He enjoyed watching her move about the kitchen. Her strawberry-blonde hair was pulled up in a messy bun, and she was wearing an old ratty robe and slippers. It didn't matter; he still found her sexy. She was an amazingly talented cook, and whatever she made, he loved. He didn't remember having ever seen her use premade mixes or boxed meals. He sat at the small island bar, sipping his coffee, and watched her crack the eggs and fry the bacon—one of his secret bad habits almost no one knew about.

"I made reservations for us at the new hotel off the river," Rachel said. "Oh, and I already reserved a car. It will be waiting for us at the airfield. I also made dinner reservations for the second night at Eddie's. You remember Eddie's, right? That's the place with the glass wine elevator. I thought the last night we could all go to a play. I was thinking of a holiday play or a holiday movie. What do you think?"

"Well, honey, you always plan the perfect trips, and this is about the family, so whatever you and the kids want to do, we do. This is the one time of the year my office absolutely will not call me for anything. One of my partners will take all my calls. And I don't have any business scheduled for Krannert." Brad got up from the table and placed both his arms around Rachel's neck, pulling her toward him. "The trip is all about us," he said, softly kissing the nape of her neck. He loved his life and his family, and he was looking forward to this trip.

...

Rachel had planned everything perfectly. Brad flew the family from Krannert to Cedar Valley, a small independent airstrip outside of New York City. Just as Rachel had arranged, the rental car was waiting for them when they landed, and the annual holiday trip began. Brad made certain everything Rachel and the children had planned and wanted to do took place. The family even stayed an extra night so they could attend a Trans-Siberian Orchestra concert. The following evening, they headed back to Cedar Valley Airport. True to his word, Brad had made sure everyone had enjoyed the perfect holiday trip.

Before leaving the hotel, Brad checked the weather report. Visibility was low, but not low enough to stop or delay flights. The skies were dark and cloudy, but he would be able to fly above the storms. Brad and Rachel loaded the hull of the plane with their purchases. As usual, the kids fought over who was going to sit where in the cabin. Stephanie, one of the twin daughters, ended up sitting in the row directly behind her dad. Her sister, Elizabeth, sat behind her mother. The boys sat in the last row of seats. Within minutes, all the kids had their ear plugs in and were either listening to music or playing games with their iPhones. Brad performed the final safety check and cleared his flight plan with air traffic control. He climbed into the cockpit, checked the instruments, turned on the engine, and just before heading down the runway, leaned over and kissed Rachel, believing his life was truly perfect.

Given the low visibility and darkening night skies, Brad knew he would need to navigate using the instruments. Barely thirty minutes into the flight, all the kids were asleep. Rachel had started off the flight reading a book, and soon she too was sound asleep. Brad settled in for a quiet three-hour flight.

Over time, visibility gradually became worse, and in the dark of the night sky, Brad didn't immediately realize how low to the ground he was. He didn't see the runway lights of Krannert until it was too late. Suddenly he realized he was only a few dozen meters above the ground and not the distance he needed to safely pull the plane up. "Jesus, no!" he yelled.

Rachel jumped at the sound of his voice and immediately realized the danger they were all in. Crying out in panic, she turned around to wake up the children. But it was already too late. The plane was tilted almost completely on the right, with the wing skimming the tall grasses next to the airstrip.

"Brad!" Rachel managed to cry out before the right side of the plane hit the ground and flipped over on itself.

When the plane finally came to a stop, it erupted in flames. Brad managed to crawl out of the pilot's seat and jump through a side window, with no choice but to leave Rachel strapped in her seat and screaming. Within seconds, the plane was engulfed in flames, and his beloved wife finally stopped screaming. Frantically crawling from the flames, Brad stopped to look back and saw Stephanie lying on the ground, several feet away, having been thrown clear during the landing from her seat directly behind his. He crawled to where she lay, assuming the worse. Just before he lost consciousness, he heard sirens.

Seven

Emily found herself thinking of the body floating in the surf. She couldn't shake the feeling that something about him was familiar. She arrived at her office earlier than normal. In this sleepy beach town, the office she purchased had regular business hours, much like a bank. However, she was accustomed to arriving by eight in the morning and leaving around six in the evening. This particular morning she arrived around seven, made a pot of coffee, and put a bagel in the toaster.

In Boston, she had been not only a successful prosecuting attorney but also the local television station's legal analyst. She gave commentaries on pending criminal cases around the country as well as local cases. The only cases she was unable to comment on were cases she herself was prosecuting. But that didn't prevent her from speaking when her cases were over, after the juries had deliberated and given their decision or after the defendant had accepted a plea bargain. She loved the camera, the attention and notoriety. It gave purpose to her life, made her feel important. She would have stayed in Boston, married Eric, kept the job, and continued with her life if it weren't for the James case and losing her friend Rachel.

The sound of the toaster popping out the bagel brought Emily back to reality. There was a killer out there who had disposed of a body on the beach, a body she had found. She was a witness. Still deep in thought, she gathered up her bagel and coffee and went back to her office to review her schedule of client meetings.

Her paralegal, Toni, would be in soon. Emily had inherited Toni when she purchased the law practice. Toni was cheerful, pleasant, and knew all the clients' cases inside and out. She was a natural at making clients feel comfortable, which was essential in aiding Emily's efforts to take over the practice. Russell White had practiced law in this town for close to forty years. He was well respected. In assuming his law practice, Emily knew she would need Toni's skills to help her succeed.

Toni entered the office's reception area, cheerfully calling out to Emily that she had brought lunch for the two of them and had already confirmed Emily's appointments for the day.

"So what is for lunch?" Emily said, relieved to see her.

Toni answered her while organizing her desk and turning on a space heater. "I made meatloaf last night—too much, as usual. I also made English toffee. I know we agreed to no sweets, but it's getting colder outside, and the candy makes the office more like home. When Mr. White was here, I always had a bowl of candy next to the coffee pot. He would have a piece of candy every morning with his coffee."

"I think the candy should remain part of the coffee routine," Emily said. "I can't wait to try the meatloaf, but first I think I should try a piece of the toffee with my coffee."

Toni eagerly opened the tin of candy and held it out for Emily to try. It was then Emily knew she had found a place she would enjoy coming to every day, and that she had a paralegal who would become more than just a valuable asset to the business. The women munched on toffee and drank the coffee Emily had made. But instead of talking about work, Emily shared the events of the evening before and explained that she thought the floater looked familiar, but she just couldn't remember why.

...

Emily stayed late at the office that evening reviewing files of current clients to familiarize herself with the cases. She reviewed the upcoming court schedule and made a list of what was needed to prepare for each hearing. When she was done, she went over the current billing and expenses. Toni had everything well organized and documented. When she was satisfied she was done for the evening, she headed home.

Emily had not wanted to draw attention to herself when she relocated to her new town. Wanting to fit in with the locals, she had traded her Mercedes SUV for a Toyota Camry. Her car was parked behind her office building. The lot was usually well lit, but tonight the lights near her car were off. In Boston, she would have had security walk her out, but not here.

As she walked toward her car, she used her key fob to unlock her car and turn on the lights. Tossing her briefcase onto the front passenger-side seat, she slid into the Camry, slowly sighing as she settled in and glanced at the windshield. Placed neatly underneath one wiper blade was a small white envelope, the type a bouquet of flowers might have. She glanced around the lot, suddenly afraid. Seeing no one, she locked the doors and slowly backed out of the space, scanning the area in front of her car to ensure no one had been hiding beneath it. When she was convinced she was alone, she parked and jumped out of the car, grabbed the envelope off the windshield, and hurriedly got back inside, locking the doors. She drove home holding the envelope.

Emily had purchased a small cottage off Hampton Beach, New Hampshire. It was in a quiet neighborhood, and most of her neighbors were of retirement age. She pulled into her garage and closed the door. Steadying her nerves, she carefully got out of her car and sprinted for the safety of her laundry room door. With the envelope still in her hand, she slammed the door shut behind her and flipped on the lights. Sighing in relief, she allowed herself to relax and finally looked at the envelope. Leaning against the door, she turned it over, examining the front and back. Nothing was written on it. She carefully opened it and pulled out a tattered, old picture of a young boy. Written in small block letters with black marker at the bottom of the picture was the name JAMES. Emily dropped the picture, watching it float to the floor.

Eight

It had been a little over a week since Emily had assumed Russell White's practice, just under a month since she had left Boston, and just one week since she had stumbled upon the body. She hadn't expected finding the body would create a problem or even cause her to feel stressed. She had seen numerous dead bodies in her career, so many that she had lost count. Death never bothered her. In fact, she saw death as a relief. The dead were no longer lonely or in pain. As far as an afterlife, she figured she would find out eventually. She didn't hold to any actual belief, other than the belief that some type of hell had to exist. Dante's vision of hell satisfied the demons that haunted her. Wandering upon this dead guy soon after moving to what she thought and hoped would be a quiet little town away from the garbage of her prior life had thrown her a curve ball.

It was close to three a.m., and she was wide awake, staring in the dark at the ceiling. Lately she had started taking Ambien to help her sleep. It worked great at first; she'd been able to sleep a few hours. But now she found herself doubling up on the dose and waking after only a couple hours of sleep. Since she was awake again now, she decided to go for a walk.

Emily lived close to the beach, actually very close to where the floater had been found. In spite of the time, the moon was full and bright, and the sky clear. She could see very well without a flashlight. She walked toward the beach, engrossed in thought, trying to convince herself the floater hadn't looked familiar. The coroner hadn't identified him yet.

No one from her previous life knew where she had moved, not even Eric. She had deleted her Facebook account and blocked every connection from her phone. Even her former coworkers knew little to nothing about her personal life, and she wanted to keep it that way. Leaving Eric was the hardest part of leaving Boston, but she had to go. After the accident, she couldn't face him without thinking that he was somehow involved.

She met Eric during her last year of law school, during a Moot Court competition. They both competed for their schools. He played the part of opposing counsel for his school, and she was on the defense team. She was instantly attracted to him. He was adorable, with his sandy-brown hair and blue eyes, but when he spoke he went from adorable to absolutely sexy. He had a slight Midwestern accent, and his voice carried nicely in the courtroom. Outside the courtroom his voice was softer, almost as if a different person were speaking. What attracted her most to him was that he was brilliant. He had been a child prodigy. He completed college and law school in record time and passed the bar exam with very little prep, when she had to study for hours. He not only knew the material but could also correctly apply it for the benefit of his clients.

Emily and Eric were inseparable during the competition, and

afterward their relationship continued to grow. Once they both passed the bar exam, they moved in together and settled into a nice routine. The eventual plan was to get married and start a family; however, they were both busy focusing on their careers. She was hired by the prosecutor's office and eventually became a legal correspondent for the local news. Eric immediately started a private law firm and spent the bulk of his free time learning to fly at Krannert. He soon became business partners with his flight instructor, Brad.

After her best friend Rachel's death, Emily wasn't able to get past a feeling that Eric either knew more than he was admitting or that he was somehow involved. This growing suspicion tore apart whatever attraction she once felt for him. In the end, the very sight of him made her ill. His voice was a constant reminder of how much her feelings had changed. The only thing she kept from their relationship was a chunky, twisted dark-gold bracelet he gave her after one of his charter flights to Italy. He told her he'd had it made for her out of a handful of gold nuggets he had purchased with his first paycheck from the charter. Leaving her practice and life behind was painful enough, but this bracelet was her last hold on her prior life and one she wasn't ready to put away. It was a reminder of how good her life had been before she allowed her career and her choices to be influenced by money and greed.

While she walked she played with the bracelet, remembering the times with Eric that had been decent, before her news anchor position, before his involvement with Brad, and before Rachel and the kids died. Eric wasn't the only one to blame for their breakup. Emily had loved her dual roles as prosecuting attorney and as a legal consultant for the local news. She loved the limelight, being the center of attention, and getting requests for her opinions, as well as being able to verbalize her opinion without being asked. She thrived on the banter between herself as a prosecutor and the defense attorneys who also served as legal counsel for the television station. Soon she became a local celebrity, which she thoroughly enjoyed. But her opinions hadn't always been factually correct, and she soon stopped caring if she was right or wrong. She was paid to give her opinion, and in law, one side always loses. Although rare, she'd had her losses, but her wins were what drove her. And when she won, she gloated.

There was one case in particular that had gained national attention and for which she had been lucky enough to be the lead prosecutor. She had gladly and eagerly held press conferences regarding "catching the deviant and obtaining his voluntary confession." After he was sentenced, she gave her opinion to anyone with a camera, but this time she was wrong. In fact, she had evidence that would have exonerated the defendant. But to her it wasn't enough. It didn't matter; she had a confession. She was completely caught up in the attention she was afforded as a celebrity.

The defendant's name was James Johnson. He was barely seventeen years old, a young, skinny white kid charged with aggravated rape of a minor. His IQ was around eighty, perhaps low but legally still average. He knew the difference between right and wrong; he knew what a lie was and that sex without consent was wrong. He even knew that sex with a minor was wrong. He admitted to all of this and was tried as an adult, found guilty, sentenced to twenty years, and placed in an adult maximum-security prison. Initially he was held in protective custody, but eventually he was moved into the general population. There he became a target and was brutally beaten, raped, and murdered. He was found crumpled at the bottom of a stairwell. His face was barely recognizable; he had numerous broken bones, stab wounds, and lacerations. Several of the wounds were postmortem. Prison officials had no explanation as to how he ended up in a stairwell. Emily didn't feel any guilt over his death; he was just one less inmate for the taxpayers to support and proof that there is justice, even in prison. But his death didn't end the case. It was just the beginning of her fall from grace, leading to her eventual feelings of remorse.

Still deep in thought about James, Emily found herself walking toward the location where the body had floated ashore. She stopped, looking across the water, and noticed how loud the ocean sounded in the silence. The water glistened in the moonlight. There simply wasn't any way she could have known this man. There could not be a connection! Yet she couldn't shake the feeling that there was something very familiar about him, that she somehow knew him. As she gazed at the water, it suddenly came to her. She *did* know him. Not personally, but professionally. He had been the police detective in Boston who had gotten the confession out of James. Or rather, he was present when James confessed.

"Connard," she barely whispered aloud. His name was Detective Connard! She did know him! She remembered when he had come to her with the signed confession. She had heard rumors that Connard was very good at getting confessions out of subjects. She didn't care how he got the confession, just that she had one. She didn't ask him about the details. She made it a point to never ask how a confession was obtained. That was the job of the defense. Once she had the confession, she quickly notified the media, held a press conference, and announced the state's position on prosecuting the defendant. She stopped all further investigations of the case and pursued James as the only suspect, and eventually the only defendant. James's entire trial, including jury deliberations, had lasted only two days. Sentencing was held thirty days later. James was found dead sixty-two days after that.

The sun was starting to come up, and Emily slowly stood and brushed sand off her legs. She had spent the better part of the early-morning hours sitting in the sand, staring at the water, thinking about James, his confession, his death, and the detective. In her core, she knew she was responsible for James's death. She had prematurely halted the investigation, prosecuted the easiest defendant to convict, and ignored the evidence that pointed in a different direction. She couldn't blame the media or the state for pushing his conviction, because they didn't. She did.

The state had wanted the right defendant convicted, not just anyone. But she had wanted to prove herself as a new prosecutor, and she had needed to be the attorney who prosecuted this case. She was elated when Detective Connard brought her the confession, and when she presented it to the press, she conveniently forgot she had exculpatory DNA evidence that not only was James innocent in this case, but that the actual offender had been arrested and charged with a different rape and murder. After James's death, the DNA evidence was leaked to the press.

In the end the Johnson family sued the state, collected a couple million, and moved away. Emily was terminated from her positions as chief prosecuting attorney for the city and legal counsel for the news program. After a year of hiding from public view, Emily purchased a law practice from a family friend who was retiring. The absolute last topic or case she wanted to remember or be reminded of now was James. She wondered if the detective's death had anything to do with James's death. But what frightened her more was the thought that finding the card on her car was somehow connected to Detective Connard and maybe even the Johnson case.

Emily turned away from the water, took her cell phone out of her pocket, and called Sheriff McNeil. He answered on the first ring. Before he could say hello she started talking, fast at first but then forcing herself to slow down. "Sheriff, I'm sorry to call you at this hour. This is Emily Bridges. I don't know if you remember me, but I'm the person who found the body on the shore."

"Uh, yeah, I remember," muttered the sheriff. "What do you want that couldn't wait until eight o'clock?"

"I need to tell you I think I know who he is. The body, that is . . . I know him." Emily paused, nervously waiting for him to say something.

After a few seconds to process this new information, he said, "OK, Counselor, who is he?"

Emily hesitated, knowing it would be hard to explain why she hadn't recognized the floater when he was found on the beach. She also knew she couldn't tell the sheriff about the photo she'd found on her windshield. If she did, he would think she was somehow involved in this murder.

"He was a police detective I once worked with. I didn't work with him directly, and only on one case. He was loosely involved in an investigation of a suspect I prosecuted," she replied.

"So, Counselor, you're telling me the body you found in the water is none other than a police detective you once worked with and knew? How did you miss this?" he yelled into the phone.

Emily tried to explain how she hadn't remembered at first that she had worked with him. "Boston is a big city with thousands of police officers. It's impossible to remember each one. Even the officers don't all know each other!" she said.

"Counselor, tell me, what case was he loosely involved with when he worked for you?" The sheriff was now fully awake, and his voice did not hide his irritation with Emily.

"Well, uh, Sheriff, he didn't work *for* me. I said he was loosely involved in a case that I managed."

"I see. My mistake, OK? Now, how about you tell me what case he was 'loosely involved' with? Can you do that, Counselor?"

Emily responded softly, "That would have been the Johnson case." She found it very difficult to say James's name.

"Let me guess: the James Johnson case? I remember that case, as do most people in this country. If I understand you, this is the police detective who acquired the 'confession' you used to convict an innocent, mentally deficient kid who was later brutally murdered, and whose family sued the city and caused you to almost lose your license to practice law. And you expect me to believe you forgot who this cop was? Lady, I am not that stupid!"

"Sheriff, I don't expect you to believe me, but if I had anything to hide, I wouldn't have called you to tell you I remembered who he was!" Emily said. "I tried very hard to forget everything about that case, the confession, and the detective. It destroyed my career and almost my life. I just wanted to move forward and put that awful part of my life behind me so I could practice law the way I first intended, with no drama and no media."

The sheriff was silent for a few seconds and then sternly replied, "I am sure James's family wishes they could move forward and put it behind them too, but they can't because their son is dead, and he didn't need to die." The line went dead.

Emily turned back toward the water. For the first time in her adult life, she didn't know what to do. Part of her wanted to call Eric and tell him everything, but she couldn't bring herself to do it. She desperately wanted someone to confide in, and with Rachel gone, there was no one. She walked back to her house still wondering if the detective's body had anything to do with the photo she had found on her car. Deep down, she knew it did. What scared her most was that she had no idea who was behind the dead body or the photo, and there was no one she could trust or turn to for help.

Nine

Mac had hung up on Emily. It was just after five a.m., and she had woken him with a ridiculous story of how she finally recognized the guy she'd found on the beach. Plus, she was connected to the body. He was pissed off. How the hell did she expect him or anyone to believe she hadn't remembered who the floater was? He had to notify the coroner, but he wasn't going to call the guy at five in the morning. He would call him later.

Unfortunately, later came faster than he would have liked. The alarm went off promptly at six; he reached over and tapped the iP-hone, instantly silencing the sound. Sitting up, he looked around his room. His house was very neat and tidy, but his bedroom was always a mess. His uniforms were tossed over a chair, and an old wooden quilt rack doubled as a clothes hanger, stacked with jeans and shirts. He used an old folding dinner tray as a nightstand. Occasionally it would collapse, spilling his cell phone and water bottle onto the floor.

Mac slowly threw his legs off the bed, rubbing his face with his hands and mulling over Emily's admission that she knew the identity of the body. He decided it was time to notify the coroner.

"This is Davis," said the voice on the other end of the phone line.

Still sleepy, Mac cleared his throat before speaking. "Yeah, Doc, good morning. It seems Emily, the new attorney in town, did know the identity of the floater. She called me a little bit ago and said his name is Detective Connard. She didn't remember his first name. Said she worked a case with him in Boston. I will contact the Boston Police Department later this morning and arrange for a positive ID of the body. Do you have a cause of death yet?"

"Actually, we do, and it's a strange one. By the way, good morning back," said Ryan Davis. "Cause of death was asphyxiation. Normally, in an asphyxiation death, the eyes will have broken vessels that indicate choking, but given the time he spent in salt water, the eyes were too degraded. Anyway, I won't bore you with all the gory details, but I have only heard of this type of case and never seen one. In fact, I wasn't even sure this was a real way to kill someone! Have you heard of burking?"

"Uh, no. What the hell is burking?" Mac walked into his kitchen to get a pot of coffee started. He was going to need the caffeine.

"We didn't see any bruising on the body, but the lungs appeared to have been deprived of oxygen. It appears his death was caused by burking. The first recorded cases originally began in the early 1800s. In Scotland there were several murders committed by smothering the victims by pushing the jaw upward while blocking the mouth and nose and compressing the torso at the same time. This has the same effect as choking, but it doesn't leave any marks or bruises. And it's also a slow death. Not a very pleasant way to die, if there is a pleasant way to die. But this method takes time and strength." He paused to allow Mac a moment to process what he was telling him.

"I remembered a professor in medical school telling a story about 'anatomy murders.' Anyway, I rechecked the body, and as it happens, this is the cause of death. It's the only thing it can be." Ryan knew the cause of death probably created more questions for the police than answers, but at least it was a start.

"OK. So, Doc, in your opinion, it would take a fairly strong person to do this, right?"

"Yes, it would, unless the victim was unable to fight back. For instance, if he was intoxicated or drugged. But this guy had a blood alcohol level of point oh four, and with a weight of one hundred eighty pounds, he wouldn't have been intoxicated, and he should have been able to fight off his attacker."

"You think a woman could have done this?" Mac asked.

"No, Mac, I seriously doubt a female could have killed this guy and then stuffed him into a

scuba suit. Well, at least not alone, anyway. Maybe if she had a partner. But, Mac, this murder was well thought out. Whoever did this knew exactly what he was doing. This wasn't a heat-of-the-moment killing, and the scuba suit just adds to the intrigue."

Mac thanked the coroner for the update and then called the Boston Police Department to notify them of the detective's death. He hadn't even had his morning coffee, and the next thing on his agenda would be to talk face-to-face with Emily. He wasn't buying her story that she had "suddenly" remembered the floater's identity. Mac planned to be at her office when she opened her door.

Ten

Emily went to the office early. She couldn't sleep, and she knew the sheriff would be stopping in. She had every intention of being ready for him and his questions. She had buried the part of her life in which Connard had played a role. He was less than a distant memory. Part of her knew Connard had coerced a confession from James, but that was in the past. She was pouring her second cup of coffee when the sheriff walked in. Figuring it would benefit her to sound positive, she greeted him warmly.

"Good morning, Sheriff. I had a feeling I would be seeing you today. Do you want any coffee?" She held out a cup.

Mac accepted the coffee and politely followed her into the conference room. He noticed she was walking more confidently than the last time he had seen her. She was dressed in a suit that accentuated her figure while also making her appear professional and a little bit cold—just the way he remembered her from her TV show. The conference room was narrow and long, with a long oval table in the center. The chairs were much too large for the room but were comfortable. On the wall facing the door was an old portrait of a young man. *Interesting painting*, Mac thought. *Not what you would think would be in a law office.* Mac waited for Emily to sit down before speaking.

"Nice painting," he said, nodding toward the wall.

"It's a print," Emily replied.

"It's a good one."

"It was a gift."

Changing the subject, Mac continued, "I am sure you know why I'm here this morning, Emily. As you know, you called me very early this morning to report that you recognized the victim who was found on the beach. When did you realize you knew the identity of the body?"

"Like I told you on the phone, I called you as soon as I realized who he was," Emily said. "I know you don't believe me, but when I worked in Boston, I didn't know all the police officers. There are hundreds. Yes, I did know a few very well, but I didn't know Connard. I only knew *of* him. And frankly, after the James case, I truly tried to forget everything, including the detective who acquired the confession, and that was Connard. We weren't exactly friends, and I never saw him outside of work. In fact, I only saw him a few times at work."

She paused to sip her coffee and then, avoiding his gaze, slowly continued. "When I first saw him lying on the sand, I thought I knew him. But I couldn't place him. Then I convinced myself I was imagining things. Have you ever met someone you thought you knew but couldn't place?"

Mac didn't answer but waited for her to continue.

"Well, that's how I felt, but after a few days I let it go. Last night

I couldn't sleep, so I went for a walk. It finally came to me who he was. I called you as soon as I remembered. That's it, nothing more."

Emily gently placed her coffee cup on the table, drawing a deep breath while folding her hands around the cup as if gaining strength from the heat of it. She looked defeated, older than her years, and worn out. Mac wasn't sure if this was the toll of the James case or her fall from grace. Maybe it was simply the effects of a sleepless night. He remembered watching her on television, her hair and clothes perfect, speaking with an arrogant tone of entitlement. She was excellent at berating the accused and equally talented at churning public outcry. Because of her, at times a case would be moved out of the area in an effort to afford the accused a fair trial. She was that good. This person sitting at the table was not the person he was used to watching. She wasn't even the person he just watched walk into the conference room. He knew her better than she thought, and he also knew this behavior was an act.

"Emily, when did you first meet Detective Connard?" he asked.

"When did I first meet him?" she asked. "I thought I already told you he was the detective who got the confession from James."

"Right. That's what you said, but that wasn't my question. Let me repeat it. When did you first *meet* Detective Connard?" He was carefully watching her reaction. The sullen attorney persona was gone, and the cold, calculating attorney was back. He wondered which personality was real.

"OK, so I knew who he was. But I didn't know him. I was never introduced to him, and I never worked directly with him. My office staff worked with him. And I'm sure you are well aware that the office of the prosecutor has a very large staff. But yes, I did know he was Detective Connard. The first time I actually spoke to him was during the James investigation. I knew the confession was suspect. I didn't care. I knew his reputation, and I knew who he was," she said while fingering her coffee cup.

"What was your relationship with Detective Connard after he

obtained the confession?" Mac said as he leaned back comfortably in the chair. His interest was more in her behavior and reaction to his questions than in the answers.

She sighed heavily before replying. "Nice try, Sheriff. There wasn't a relationship. As I told you several times, I worked with him. I did speak to him during the investigation and trial, but after James's death, when it was determined the confession was coerced, my attorney advised that I not speak to Connard. I followed that advice. There was no relationship. If you are suggesting I slept with him, let me clear that one up. He wasn't my type. I have a habit of not associating with the people I work with, and that included other staff who worked with the prosecutor's office. And I sure as hell didn't sleep with cops, no offense intended.

"Other than that, I did run into him once at a pub. He was at a small table, sitting alone, and he was drinking something. I didn't ask. We exchanged pleasantries, and that was all. I was meeting an associate at the pub and was in a hurry."

Mac continued to watch her, trying to decipher if she was telling the truth or creating a story she thought he would buy. "OK, well, if you can think of anything else I need to know, please call the office. Otherwise, I think I am finished for now. And no need to concern yourself with offending me," Mac said as he pushed his chair back to get ready to leave.

Mac was almost out the door when Emily stood and faced him.

"Make no mistake, Sheriff," she said with the cold, calculated tone he'd heard her use countless times on TV, "I had nothing to do with Connard's death. I may have known of him, may have even worked with him, but that's all. There's no mystery here. I would advise you not to make one, either. My stumbling upon his body was nothing more than mere coincidence. Whether you choose to believe that or not is on you."

Mac nodded and responded just as icily, "Make no mistake, Emily, I don't believe in coincidences. There is a reason why that particular detective's body washed up on our beach. Not to mention how close to your new home it happened. Maybe your finding him was just a fluke, but he was there for a reason. And I will find out. I don't make up facts to fit circumstances. If I recall, that's *your* method, isn't it? And by the way, you met with Connard more than once, and it wasn't in passing at a pub. I have my own sources, Counselor. And mine do not fabricate facts or events." With that, he left her silently standing in the doorway.

She longed to call Eric, to tell him what she'd found, to ask him for help. But she couldn't. She watched the sheriff leave, and she had no doubt he would be back.

Eleven

Growing up as a child prodigy in a wealthy family, Eric had always been showered with attention from his family and friends. Whatever he did, he did it better than most. After law school, he excelled with his practice, but he quickly became bored with practicing law and needed another outlet for his energy. As a surprise gift, Emily purchased flying lessons for Eric at Krannert Airport. Eric's flying instructor was a guy named Brad who was also an MD. Eric and Brad discovered they had a lot more in common than the love of flying and quickly became good friends. Through them, Rachel and Emily became friends. In the beginning, the couples did almost everything together, from dinners and movies to vacationing. Eric continued taking flying lessons until he earned his pilot's license.

Eric was always high-energy. Flying provided a great outlet for his drive, plus it allowed him the freedom to come and go as he needed without being accountable to Emily. He guarded his private life with a vengeance, and being in a relationship meant that most of his life was open to Emily. Flying gave him the privacy and freedom he craved. Krannert's International Charter Service was born of both Eric's and Brad's love of flying and their mutual need to escape the daily grind of a regular nine-to-five job. It also provided an escape from the women in their lives, not to mention a damn good income. Brad and Eric made sure one of them was always either at the airport or accessible by phone for their clients. They each had their own small private jet that could carry six people comfortably, and their charter service had one luxury jet, owned by Krannert, that had a nice cargo hold and could carry several people.

Brad and Eric both craved adventure and excitement, and Krannert's International Charter Service, with exclusive private clients, gave them a reason to leave and an excuse to play. Their initial clients were wealthy men who enjoyed private flights out of the country for vacations, quick flights for business, or an occasional private flight with a mistress. The charter service soon became very profitable, and both men were looking forward to the day they could leave their day-to-day jobs behind and only fly for select clients.

Twelve

Brad woke up in intensive care. The last thing he remembered was leaving the hotel with his family. He looked around the room and recognized the equipment. In the corner of the room next to the door, Eric was sleeping in a chair. Brad felt his chest and discovered he had leads attached for the cardiac monitor. He had an IV and a capped arterial line. He tried to find the call light, but he couldn't reach it. *Typical*, he thought. *Nurses always forget to give the patients the call lights.* He tried to speak but wasn't able to do much more than emit a weak cough. After what seemed like hours but was more like a few minutes, the nurse walked into the room.

"Dr. Rivers, glad to see you're awake. I'm Kelly, your nurse today. Do you know where you are?"

Brad just looked at her, since he was too weak to speak.

"Dr. Rivers, you were in a plane accident. You were brought

here from the accident site, which was right outside of Reagan, New Hampshire. You're at St. Luke's Hospital in Boston, in the ICU burn unit. The ICU doctor will be in here soon to speak with you."

Brad tried to respond, his brain scrambling to put the pieces together. How did he get in a plane accident, and where was his family? Why didn't she mention his family?

Within minutes a physician entered the room. "Brad, it's good to see you awake. I am Dr. Shah, one of the ICU physicians."

Brad listened to Dr. Shah tell him he had sustained second-degree burns to his right arm and the right side of his face and torso, and third-degree burns to his right hand. All the wounds would heal with only minimal scarring. Brad slowly began to understand that the plane he and his family were in had crash-landed on their way home from their annual holiday trip. Dr. Shah didn't mention his family; just that there had been an accident.

Eric was standing next to the doctor, looking at the floor. Brad was afraid to ask, to even think about where his family was. His mind was racing; he was barely keeping up with what he was hearing. All he could think about was Rachel and the kids.

"So, Brad," said Dr. Shah, "I think you can be transferred to the progressive care side of the burn unit. The physical therapists and the wound team will continue to manage the dressing changes, and if all goes well, you could be discharged in a few days."

Dr. Shah finished a quick assessment of his dressings as he spoke and then hurriedly left the room. The nurse had already left. Brad found it odd that no one had asked if he was in pain.

Eric cleared his throat and began to softly explain what had happened. It seemed that on landing Brad had lost control of the plane and crashed into a field a few miles from Krannert. Given the rain and limited visibility, the National Transportation Safety Board's initial assessment was instrument failure or pilot error. Brad's wife, Rachel, and their sons had died on impact. Only one of the twin girls survived. She was in the pediatric unit with minor injuries. On impact the plane had ignited. Somehow Stephanie escaped without any burns. As he listened to Eric telling him how his family had died, how his beautiful wife had been burned beyond recognition, his sons and one daughter dead, Brad felt his perfect life crumbling.

"Brad, I am so sorry. I know this is a lot to digest, but I will be here to help you through this. Whatever you need, I am here," said Eric. "We are friends and business partners, but I am also your attorney. Unfortunately, I have to advise you that you may want to seek different counsel. But if you don't, and if you want me to remain your attorney, then we have to go over what happened. The sooner the better. I know this is early, but we have to deal with the NTSB. Your pilot's license has already been suspended pending further investigation into the cause of the accident. As you know, this is standard. I will do whatever you want or need to clear this up, but the investigation could take several months. I have already submitted the plane's maintenance records and safety logs, along with your flight records and physical. While the investigation is ongoing, you won't be able to fly. It's possible you could permanently lose your license, although you probably don't want it back anyway. We can make arrangements if you want to either sell Krannert or sell the charter or simply close it down. We can do whatever you want."

Brad was looking out the window while Eric spoke, and Eric wasn't sure he was listening. Maybe it was still too early for him to process the loss. Then suddenly Brad spoke.

"I am not losing my license, Krannert, or the charter! You do whatever you need to maintain my license. I have lost everything else, and I am not losing that!"

Eric assured Brad he would do everything possible to save his license. Even though he was surprised at Brad's response, he didn't pass judgment. People respond differently to tragedy. Brad had just been told what had happened, and the process of dealing with the deaths and guilt would come later.

Before Eric left the hospital, he stopped by the pediatric unit to see Stephanie. She looked remarkably like her mother. She was sitting up in bed, talking with her maternal grandparents. Eric gave her a stuffed toy he had purchased from the gift shop. Even though she had just lost her twin sister, her brothers, and her mother, Stephanie didn't seem sad.

Thirteen

During his visit with Brad, Eric had received a phone call from the NTSB investigator asking to meet with him at Krannert. Eric readily agreed.

The airfield was just west of town, a quick twenty-minute drive from the hospital. The airport was used mostly for crop-dusting and for private pilots who flew recreationally and had small single- or double-engine aircrafts. There were several hangars the airfield rented out, as well as one maintenance hangar and one small terminal that housed business offices. Eric parked at the terminal and walked briskly into his office. The investigator was waiting for him at his office door, holding an empty coffee mug.

"I'm Eric Wilkerson, Dr. Rivers's attorney and general counsel for Krannert's Airfield," Eric said as he approached. "Whatever you need, I'm sure we can get it for you quickly. I have already instructed the staff to provide access to whatever you request."

"Henry Mills," the investigator said as he reached out to shake Eric's hand.

Mills had a slight build and appeared fit. He looked to be in his sixties.

Eric opened his office door and gestured toward the chairs that sat across from his desk, before slowly taking his own seat. Too late, he realized he should have offered the investigator coffee or water. His mind was still on his conservation with Brad.

"I retired from the airlines as a commercial pilot about five years ago," Mills began, "and started working with the FAA in the NTSB as an investigator. My office handles not only accidents but near misses and in-air violations, as well as overseeing pilot licensure issues. The investigative process for a crash takes several months, as we have to wait for the determination of the cause, which involves an extensive exam into the craft itself. We also look at the medical records of the pilot and the flight plan submitted prior to takeoff. We don't look to place blame. Our goal is to determine the cause and prevent future accidents. Sometimes these small crafts have problems that need to be addressed to prevent another tragedy, and sometimes pilot error is the cause. As part of the process, we have suspended Dr. Rivers's license. Of course, he may continue to operate as the general manager of Krannert's Airfield. However, he can't fly locally or internationally. I understand the two of you are co-owners in a charter service."

Eric nodded. "Yes, we are co-owners and partners."

"You are also a pilot."

Eric nodded in response. "Mr. Mills, let me reassure you that whatever you need from the business or my office will be provided to you. Dr. Rivers's records are open for your review, as is the service record of the plane. I do need to stress that Dr. Rivers's end goal is to retain his license. It's very important for this business and for Dr. Rivers to reclaim his life."

...

Brad went back to work almost immediately following the funerals and then sent Stephanie to a private boarding school in Boston. He also confirmed to Eric that he had no intention of giving up his license to fly and would do anything necessary to keep it, telling his partner it was the only thing he had left from his former life, and after losing everything else that mattered to him, he wasn't going to lose that too. He even hired two more physicians to cover his practice so he could spend more time at Krannert.

Within a few months of the deaths of his family, Brad met Beverly. She and her children brought meaning back into his life, and when he introduced them all to Stephanie, the group became an instant family. Stephanie and Beverly quickly bonded as stepmother and stepdaughter, and Brad quickly found himself enjoying being a father to Beverly's children.

The couple married privately in Vegas within a year of the accident. Instead of announcing his marriage to his colleagues, friends, and family, Brad simply began referring to Beverly as his wife instead of his girlfriend. His former wife's family and friends quickly distanced themselves from both Brad and Stephanie. Rumors continued to grow about whether Brad and Beverly had been having an affair at the time of Rachel's death, and some even boldly wondered if the plane crash had truly been an accident.

The investigation into the cause of the accident took roughly one year, and as Eric had suspected, the cause was pilot error. After the investigation, Brad took remedial fight instructions and managed to regain his license. Eric was surprised at not only how determined Brad had been at working toward recovery of his license, but also at how fast he had adjusted to the loss of his family. He had heard the rumors that Brad had been having an affair at the time of the accident, but he easily dismissed them. He knew firsthand how much Brad had treasured Rachel, and as busy as Brad was, Eric couldn't imagine where he would have found the time for a mistress. He remained steadfast in his defense of his friend, even though it cost him his relationship with his fiancée, Emily.

...

Brad moved Beverly and her children into the same house he had shared with Rachel and their children. He was sitting at the kitchen bar drinking his morning coffee, thinking of his first wife, Rachel, when Beverly came in. Rachel had been an amazing cook and loved to be in the kitchen, but Beverly could barely make a hardboiled egg. Her idea of a good breakfast was cold cereal and toast or a piece of fruit.

"Do you want me to make you something to eat before you go into work?" Beverly asked cheerfully. She knew he would say no. He always did, and to be honest, she really didn't have any plans to make him breakfast. She also knew he preferred his first wife's cooking to hers. That didn't matter; what she and Brad shared was completely different from what he'd had in his first marriage. She adored him, and she knew he adored her. He and Stephanie had even started attending Sunday Mass with her.

Brad and his first wife had attended Mass occasionally, usually on holidays and special occasions. Rachel had been raised Catholic, and even though she hadn't kept up with the Church, her dream vacation was a trip to the Vatican, so Brad had taken her. According to Brad, the trip was not just a surprise for his first wife, it was the start of his charter service. Beverly was also Catholic. She adored Brad, and attending Mass as a family intensified her belief that she and Brad were meant to be together.

Brad shook his head and smiled at his wife. "No, thanks, love. I will grab something on the way to the office. I'm going to Krannert this morning and then the practice later in the day. I have just one case this afternoon. Oh, before I go, where are you with planning the family Labor Day vacation trip?"

Beverly sat down at the bar next to him and playfully slapped his thigh. "Well, now, I haven't made all the arrangements, but the cleaners will be getting the beach house ready. I have purchased the Disney passes, and today I will make the dinner reservations. If there is any place in particular you want to go, let me know."

She waited for a response, but Brad just sipped his coffee and stared into the kitchen.

"Honey, did you hear me?" she asked.

"Ugh, yes, I heard you," he said, finally glancing her way. "I don't have any preference where we eat. Maybe see where the kids want to go, or you pick the place. I'm sure wherever we go, it will be fine. This trip will be one to remember, trust me." He leaned over and kissed the top of her head before heading to the garage to get in his car.

Beverly listened to his car pull out of the garage as she shook off the feeling that something wasn't right. She knew Rachel had always planned the family trips to perfection. She wasn't Rachel, but she wanted to make Brad happy, so she instantly set about finalizing the Labor Day weekend trip.

...

Brad stopped off to grab a quick cup of coffee at a gas station on his way to Hart's. His true passion was flying and keeping the small airfield from closure. The cost to run and keep open the airfield was massive. He was very successful in obtaining endowments from individuals and groups to help with the expenses, but the economy was in a slump, and this year was particularly tight. The airfield was doing well, but if the slump continued, Brad was worried it would suffer. And closing it due to low revenue wasn't an option.

Since it was Labor Day weekend, Brad and his family were planning to fly to their home in Florida. The trip was part vacation and part work, as he had plans to meet with possible investors for the airfield. Eric had prepared the financial portfolio for Krannert and included a few generic contracts just in case Brad was able to make a deal. Beverly had made all the arrangements for their mini-vacation, just as Rachel had always made their vacation plans. He loved that all he had to do was fly the plane.

...

The family vacation went well. Everyone had a great time, and Brad made sure everyone did or got what they wanted. When it was time to head home, the family left early on a beautiful, sunny day in Palm Beach. The flight forecast called for clear skies all the way to Reagan, New Hampshire. Although it was chillier in Reagan, the weather was almost perfect.

Brad's family arrived at the airfield for the departure, excited and all talking at once. Brad had fueled the small jet, submitted his flight plan, and completed the safety checks before his wife and children boarded the plane. The boys boarded the jet first, followed by the family's cocker spaniel. Stephanie got into the jet last, buckled herself in, and immediately put on her headphones. She closed her eyes and began listening to music. Just before takeoff, Brad leaned over and kissed Beverly on the cheek.

Fourteen

It was only Tuesday, and Eric was already tired. With Brad out of the state over the long weekend, Eric had decided to get out of town himself. Unlike his partner, Eric didn't like to fly his own plane when he went on vacation or took small trips. He liked to get in and get out of the airports. Doing safety checks, submitting a flight plan, and waiting on approval to take off and land just consumed too much time. The weekends always went by too fast, even long holiday weekends like this one. Soon it was time to go back to work. Eric took the earliest flight home and went directly to his office from the airport.

He liked to get to his office early before the staff arrived. As soon as he walked in, he flipped on the news, made coffee, and scoured the break room for something to eat. After finding a protein bar and pouring his coffee, he began the task of reviewing the weekend arrest reports to determine whether the state would pursue charges, reduce charges, or simply release the arrestees if there wasn't enough evidence to convict. Occasionally a police officer would get a little overzealous, make an arrest, and write up charges that wouldn't hold.

Eric was reviewing the reports, drinking his coffee, and listening to the news when he heard the report of a small private jet crashing into a hangar at a private airfield just east of Palm Beach, Florida. The plane was piloted by an MD from New Hampshire who had taken his family on vacation. There was only one survivor, the pilot. The pilot was airlifted to a trauma center near the airstrip. Barely breathing, Eric slowly raised his eyes to the television in the corner of his office and saw images of the crash site. Even though the news did not give the name of the pilot or the deceased, Eric instantly recognized the aircraft. He didn't need to hear the rest. It was Brad. He sat frozen to his chair, the arrest reports forgotten, his brain scrambling to make sense of another crash.

Eric made a quick call to his legal secretary and his assistant to tell them he was going to Palm Beach to see a client. It was the truth; Brad was his client. Eric's assistant, Scott Thames, had recently passed the bar exam. He had also been employed as an investigator for the prosecutor's office for the past few years. Scott had attended law school part-time while working for Eric, and even though he was a new attorney, he was well versed in the court process and could manage the caseload. Eric would be available by phone if needed.

He was out of his office and on the interstate in minutes, heading back to the airport. No need to pack: his luggage from his weekend trip was still in the trunk of his car.

During his trip, he answered several calls pertaining to the crash. Even though the news had not released the name of the pilot, the air traffic controllers at Krannert, as well as those at the airfield in Florida, knew who he was. Eric tried not to think about what the NTSB, Brad's friends and colleagues, and the media would be considering—that Brad had intentionally crashed the plane. There had been speculation about the first crash, but with Emily's help, Eric had proved the first crash was simply an unfortunate accident caused by rain, poor visibility, and Brad's mistake in reading the instruments. It happens. But now, with this new accident, even Eric had misgivings about his friend.

Brad was a superb pilot. He flew one of the best small jets on the market, and he didn't make mistakes. Or if he did make a mistake, he didn't repeat it a second time. The first accident happened during a rain storm at night, but this time the sky had been clear, the weather and visibility were very good, and they had taken off during early-morning hours. It had literally been perfect flight weather. Why did Brad turn the jet around after takeoff? Why was he trying to land after taking off, and how did he miss the landing strip? An immediate landing after takeoff was an elementary skill. Eric had to wonder if Brad was skilled enough to plan and carry out two plane crashes in which everyone died except himself. Brad knew that airfield; he had flown into it several times a year over the past decade. However, Eric still wasn't ready to accept that Brad intentionally crashed his jet. The question he was fighting to ignore was whether Brad was suicidal and had intended to take himself out with this family—or he had intended to kill just his family and walk away.

He arrived at the hospital around five p.m. and quickly walked through the front door to the information desk. He gave the receptionist his name and asked for his friend's room number.

"He's in room six thirty," said the receptionist. "Take the elevator to the right of this hall, and check in with the nurses' station once you get to the unit."

The nurses' station was in the center of the unit. Eric was confused; this didn't look like a critical care unit. It looked more like a rehab floor. He approached the nurses' desk.

"Do you have a Brad Rivers on this unit? I was told by registration he was in six thirty. What type of unit is this?" he asked as he looked around.

The older woman sitting behind the desk had gray hair and glasses that rested on the edge of her nose. She quickly glanced at a computer screen and then raised her head so she could see him over the glasses. "This is a medical unit. You can go into the room. I think he is sitting in a chair."

Eric looked at her in surprised silence. How could Brad have survived a second crash that killed his entire family yet not be injured?

The door to room 630 was slightly ajar, and as he approached, Eric heard Brad talking on the phone.

"Yes, I'm fine. Just a few scratches."

Eric entered the room without knocking. Brad glanced up at him, and for a second Eric thought he looked surprised to see him, but then his friend gave him a thin smile and continued talking on the phone. He motioned for Eric to sit down. He didn't look upset. In fact, he seemed cheerful and content.

Eric walked to the side of the bed closest to where Brad was sitting. "What happened?" he asked softly, sitting on the bed, after Brad had hung up the phone.

Shaking his head and sighing, Brad answered, "I don't know. We were on our way back. You know, just a weekend trip to Florida to spend some time at the beach house and a couple days at Disney, maybe do a little shopping. Something happened during takeoff. I don't know what, but something went wrong with the controls. I think maybe the engine stalled. Somehow, I lost power. I turned the plane and tried to glide back onto the landing strip, but I missed it and hit a hangar. I really don't know what caused it, just that it happened. I was told my family didn't make it. I am still trying to wrap my head around this. I just don't understand what happened. I think I am either the unluckiest man alive or God has some strange, cruel plans for me. He spared me again. Did they tell you my family died?" Brad said absently.

Eric watched his friend's eyes and realized his reaction to the loss of his second family was shockingly flat. He was distant and unemotional. He spoke as if he had anticipated the question and rehearsed his answers.

"Eric, I will need you to represent me again. I don't want to lose anything more than I have already. You know how important the charter service is to me. I believe you know how important it is to us and our partnership."

"OK, Brad, slow down. We first have to deal with the local police and of course the FAA and the NTSB again. They will investigate, and this time I am fairly certain you will lose your license. I am not even sure if you will be allowed to operate Krannert this time." He could see his friend was becoming angry the longer he spoke.

Brad leaned over and spoke in a low, controlled voice. "I don't think you understand the implications here, Eric. We aren't losing the charter business. We have clients who rely on us, and let's be honest with each other: we rely on them too. In other words, you do whatever you have to do to protect the business, and that includes my license."

"How can you possibly be worried about the business and your license?" Eric said. "Do you hear yourself?" Eric wanted to shout at him but had to keep his voice low. "Seriously, your wife, her children, and yours and Rachel's daughter are dead! Hell, even the damn dog is dead! What's wrong with you?"

Brad sat unmoving in his chair, his legs crossed, and turned his head to look squarely at Eric. "Don't ever again ask me what is wrong with me," he said icily. "There is nothing wrong with me. Last I checked you are not a physician, you are my attorney and my business partner, and you have a job to do. That's what I pay you for, and that's what Krannert pays you to do, so do it. I want that airfield funded by the end of the year, if I have to fund it myself. As for losing my family, don't begin to imagine how I feel. I am coping the best way I know how, which is to focus on business. Just because you don't see me crying or upset doesn't mean I'm not upset. If you have any reservations about the business, I suggest you think about Tedesco and what happens when he doesn't get the services he pays for. And, Eric, don't ever question me again."

Eric slowly stood up and spoke quietly into his friend's right ear. "Brad, I don't know what exactly is going on, and I have no idea how you managed to crash another plane, but this puts us in a very tight situation. Just as you have pointed out, we have clients who have already paid, and we can't back out of Tedesco's deal. I don't need to think about Tedesco. I am well aware of who he is and what he is. We have a deadline that can't be missed. If I could, I would quit. Whatever the problem was, we could have fixed it. Your family didn't need to die. My God, Brad, Stephanie didn't have to die!"

Gesturing at Eric to sit back down, Brad answered, "Sit down, and stop the grandiose act. You don't care who dies as long the business continues and the money flows. So stop the act."

Brad sighed and waited for Eric to sit back down. "Good. Now we have work to do, and I am not referring to the NTSB. I don't give a shit what they think they know. I am not losing my license, and we aren't losing Krannert or the charters. I am sure you are aware, Eric, that everyone has a price." Brad paused, watching Eric's reaction. "We just need to find the right price and the right person."

"Fine, Brad. I will fix your mess. But once we are done with this next charter, I am out. No more of this shit. We have each made a lot of money, and I don't need any more. You need to find another pilot if you want to continue the charter."

Brad nodded. "Make sure you notify Emily. I will give her a call in a few days. It wouldn't be good if she were to find out watching the news."

"Do you want to listen to the conversation?" Eric responded.

"Sure, that will probably be the best step so our stories are the same. Go ahead and call her."

...

Eric and Emily had been classmates and friends in high school. They lost touch with one another during undergraduate school but quickly reconnected during law school. Learning came easy for him; it always had. He knew she was smart, but the material was not as easy for her. Every time he saw her, she was studying, whether it was in the law library or sitting outside on a bench in the courtyard. While other law students gathered at the Legal Beagle to drink beer and argue over case briefs, Emily was studying.

Eric and Emily separated after law school when their careers took two sharply different directions. Even though they lived only a few hours apart, they barely spoke after that. Now he needed to talk to her about the second accident.

At one time, they had all been friends. He and Emily often spent weekends with Brad and Rachel. Emily and Rachel were close, and her death was difficult for Emily. After the first accident, Emily had suspicions that Brad had intentionally crashed the plane, but Eric convinced her it was just an unfortunate accident. Not too long after, Emily took a position in Boston and left.

Eric had followed Emily's career in Boston and was disappointed at how she had become the poster child for bad lawyering. He knew her better than most, and this loud, unfeeling, and uncaring legal analyst was not the person he once knew. He had often thought of reaching out to her to see if she needed anything, but he didn't. He couldn't.

Her phone rang twice before she answered. "Hello."

Eric stammered for a moment before managing to say, "Emily? This is Eric. I know it's been a while, but something has happened, and I didn't want you to hear it on the news. I wanted to tell you myself."

When she didn't answer, he pressed his cell phone closer to his ear and could hear her breathing.

Finally she said, "Eric? I don't know what to say. It's been a long time. What's wrong? Is something wrong?"

Eric slowly explained the latest plane crash involving Brad. As he spoke, he could hear her softly crying. When he finished, he apologized. She had been right from the beginning. But he couldn't have done anything to prevent the first crash, and he couldn't have prevented the second crash, either. All he could do now was try to distance himself, and he seriously doubted that was even possible. Brad and Eric were both under contract with Tedesco, and Eric knew there was no way out unless the monsignor didn't need them anymore.

Fifteen

Seth's desire to kill wasn't fueled by the need to rectify a wrong. He didn't see himself as a vigilante. He didn't care about any particular crime or type of crime. He didn't care about his victims, either. Although his first kill as a child had been purely by accident, he was surprised by the way he felt afterward. He liked the feeling, and that was simply the reason he'd continued to kill.

Seth couldn't blame his desire or his actions on abusive or overly permissive parents. He'd had a wonderful childhood. His parents had been wealthy, educated, attentive, and loving. He wasn't a loner; he'd had friends throughout school. Only one person had known his secret, and that person was dead. He'd stopped killing after college for no particular reason; he just wasn't getting the rush he had gotten when he was younger. Not to mention he wasn't interested in getting caught and ending up in prison. However, eventually it was time to start killing again, and he'd looked forward to again feeling the rush that came with controlling whether someone lived or died.

Seth had decided Detective Connard would be the first. He had deserved to die. Picking him was easy. The guy was a pompous, arrogant ass, and he made other good cops look bad. He bullied and abused people to get their confessions. Not only was he a lousy cop, he was a lousy husband who beat his wife whenever he got drunk. Seth truly didn't think anyone would really miss Connard, not even his wife. He had been curious to see just how long it would take the coroner to identify the detective's body and whether Connard's wife would report him as missing. But the only thing Seth had known for certain before the kill was the name of his victim, and when and how he would kill him.

He also knew Connard wouldn't be the last.

Sixteen

It was late in the afternoon, and Seth was still working. The office was quiet, and he had several things to complete before he could leave. The television in the office break room was broadcasting the national news. He was focused on the organized pile of reports in front of him when the news reporter mentioned a name that brought him to his feet.

"Dr. Bradley Rivers crash-landed into a hangar, killing his second wife, her two children, and his daughter. Dr. Rivers survived this crash, which is similar to a plane crash he survived three years earlier."

Seth came from around his desk and walked into the break room. The news was showing a photo of Dr. Rivers, his latest late wife, and her two children. They had been an attractive family, just as Rivers's first family had been.

"According to the FAA, the first accident Dr. Rivers survived was a result of pilot error. Dr. Rivers misread the instruments, causing him to miss the landing strip. In this current horrific accident, an undisclosed source stated that Dr. Rivers told local authorities the engine stalled, which caused him to attempt to turn the plane around and land at the airport he had just left."

Seth didn't believe what he was hearing. Two very similar accidents, and each accident had killed Dr. Rivers's wife and children. This accident managed to kill the surviving daughter from his first marriage, too. Seth wondered what the odds were of a pilot surviving two plane crashes in which passengers were killed.

Under the Freedom of Information Act, Seth was able to access the archives of the FAA's NTSB. It wasn't hard to locate the first accident report or the decision of the FAA. The report indicated that Dr. Rivers had not misread the instruments, as the news had reported, but that he did not have enough fuel to reach the airport. According to the report, FAA regulations required an aircraft to have enough fuel to reach not only its destination airport but also an alternate airport. This safety measure was designed to ensure the plane had enough fuel to circle if needed or to land at an alternate airstrip should something unforeseen happen. According to the accident report, Rivers had intentionally removed fuel to add shopping items his wife had purchased. Fuel weighs a lot more than shopping bags. Seth wondered exactly what his wife's purchases had been that required such risk and if she had been aware of the choice. With the money the good doctor had, why hadn't he shipped the items instead of risking running out of fuel?

As he skimmed the accident report, Seth recognized another name: attorney Eric Wilkerson. He knew Eric was an attorney, but he wasn't aware he had a relationship with Dr. Rivers. He wondered if Eric was still Rivers's attorney and if he would be assisting in this new accident investigation.

It was dark when he had finished downloading and reading all the documents. He turned off the television in the break room and the lights to the office, locked the doors, and went home. He was already planning his next kill, and he knew how he was going to do it. The stirring of excitement he felt as he developed his plan was better than he had ever felt before.

Seventeen

Seth always watched or listened to the news before going to work. The evening before, he had spent hours researching the FAA records. He felt it was important—even necessary—to be aware of current world events as well as local events. His home was small and decorated with a modern flair: hardwood floors, sparse furniture, and wall hangings or pictures on painted white walls. He had one flat-screen television hanging on the wall of his living room. He listened to the news while getting ready for work. The usual weather and local news was playing, but he was waiting to hear the national news. He was curious if Dr. Rivers had been charged or was going to be charged with killing his wife and children. He never doubted the good doctor had intentionally caused the first crash.

Finally an update to the plane crash appeared on the ticker tape under the picture: FAA CONTINUES TO INVESTIGATE

CAUSE OF CRASH. PILOT STATED HE ATTEMPTED TO TURN THE PLANE AND GLIDE TO A LANDING AFTER THE PLANE LOST POWER. AT THIS TIME NO CHARGES TO BE FILED. Seth slowly nodded his head and turned off the TV. That was interesting. He had expected something more, but that was it. Not another mention of the crash, and no comparison to the first crash.

He remembered Dr. Rivers and the first accident. That accident had changed his life forever. Nothing was the same after. But this latest accident also had his attention. A few years ago, the plane crash in which Dr. Rivers's wife and children had perished, leaving only the pilot and his daughter Stephanie, was the biggest news story in Boston, as well as most of the Northeast. Seth knew from watching the news about the plane accidents that Boston's former prosecutor Emily Bridges had a connection with Rachel, Dr. Rivers's first wife. He also knew that her former lover was Dr. Rivers's attorney and close friend, Eric Wilkerson. As a prosecutor, Emily had an opportunity at one time to seek charges against Rivers for the first accident that claimed Rachel and three of her children. But there wasn't enough public interest, and nothing came of the accident. But Seth understood how difficult it would be to prove Rivers had intentionally crashed a plane while he and one child survived. The doctor had gone on with his life, fought to keep his pilot's license, and, with the help of Eric, succeeded. He remarried and somehow managed to survive yet another plane crash where he again was the pilot and his wife, her children, and Rachel's surviving daughter died. He wondered what Emily thought now, and what her former fiancé, Eric, thought.

It didn't matter what they thought now. While he finished watching the morning news, he was thinking of his next kill. He never thought of his kills as victims. In his earlier days, he only killed people no one would miss. Now that he was older, he was looking forward to killing more prominent people. He wondered if the authorities would ever connect him to his latest kills. The thought of being in the midst of an investigation and yet being completely invisible was exciting to him. That feeling he longed for was back. And he really didn't think anyone would miss his next kill.

Seth wasn't the only own watching the morning news. Brad Rivers was also intently watching the news while waiting for his hospital discharge instructions. He too noticed that the media did not compare the prior accident to this accident. The media did mention the first one, but only in passing.

Brad was being discharged from the hospital after only a few days, having survived with minor injuries. As soon as his paperwork was completed, he took a cab to the airport and purchased a ticket to fly back to Boston. While he was waiting on his flight, he checked in with his office and was surprised when his staff told of the numerous flowers and condolences that had arrived in his absence. He asked his staff to cancel his appointments for the week, thinking it was best he seemed to be taking time to mourn the loss of his wife and children. In reality, he didn't care. Beverly was an idiot, and he couldn't stand her boys. Maybe it would have been better if Stephanie hadn't been on the trip, but it was a holiday and he couldn't find a way to exclude her. He might miss her, but he was certain he would overcome the death just as he had overcome the deaths of her mother and siblings. After checking in with his office, he placed his second call. The phone rang only twice, and the voice at the other end of the phone was hesitant but excited to hear from him.

"Hi, Brad."

Brad paused for a moment before answering. "Are you alone?"

"Yes, I am now. I just stepped out of the office. I've been so worried. I tried calling several times, but it always went to voice-mail," Claire answered.

Brad ignored her concern. "Claire, I'm glad you answered my call. I need you to listen to me."

"Of course I'll listen. Whatever you need, just tell me!"

"I'm going to be out of the office for at least a week. I need to make funeral arrangements. I think it is best if we do not speak to each other for a while. I will see you at the office for business only. I expect you to abide by my wishes. I am sure you can understand how this would look if I am linked with you so quickly after losing my wife. I'll call you when I think enough time has passed. You are not to contact me under any circumstances. I want to make that clear. Do not contact me under any circumstances."

Claire didn't respond. She had expected to remain quietly by his side. No one would need to know or even suspect that his office manager was also his lover, but to be told he wanted no contact other than professionally was gut-wrenching for her.

"OK," she said quietly. "I'll wait. I won't contact you."

Before she could say goodbye, Brad hung up, leaving her standing outside the office, fighting back tears.

His next call was to his first wife's best friend and Eric's former fiancée, Emily. After Rachel died, Emily had made attempts to remain close with Stephanie. He was certain Eric had probably called her, but she would be suspicious if he didn't call her with the news that Stephanie was on the flight and didn't make it off this time. Her cell rang a couple of times and then went immediately to voice mail. He left her a short message, telling her of the accident and Stephanie's death, and asked her to call him. He knew she wouldn't call back, and he didn't care.

His flight was boarding, and Brad was excited to be heading back to Boston. He knew the NTSB would be investigating the crash, his flight records, and the plane's mechanical records. He was in for a battle with them since this was a second crash. He didn't care how long it would take to go through the investigative process. He would pay whatever fines they imposed, take remedial courses, participate in medical exams, and eventually gain his license back.

He stood quietly in line preparing to board, thinking of how his life would be different. He had loved Rachel, and of course he had loved his children, so he'd been surprised at how he didn't miss any of them after the first crash. He supposed he wouldn't miss Stephanie either. He didn't miss her now, and if he did, it wouldn't last. He had liked his second wife, Beverly, but he hadn't loved her. He loved money more, and he loved his independence. He had no intention of parting with either. Besides, when you were a doctor and a successful businessman, there wasn't a shortage of available women willing to do whatever was needed to gain your affection and your wallet.

He would need to end it with Claire. Fortunately, they had never been seen in public together; all of their liaisons had been in the office, either after hours or before hours. He was very careful. No text messages or emails. He only called her on the office cell phone, and he kept the calls short. In fact, Brad was always careful. He didn't do anything without considering all the possible outcomes.

Once in the air, Brad ordered a gin and tonic. He quickly drank it and then settled in to take a nap.

Eighteen

Emily was in her office when Brad called her. She recognized the number, but after a few rings she let it go to voice mail. *What did he want?* she wondered. She already knew about the accident. Eric had called her. Trying to keep her composure, she finally listened to his message.

She had known Rachel, Brad's first wife, for several years. She remembered meeting her after one of Eric's flying lessons. Eric had become friends with his instructor, who was an MD who just also happened to have a pilot's license. Besides being a flight instructor, Brad was also part owner of a small airstrip for private pilots. Eric and Brad had arranged for the two women to meet, and as they expected, the women became instant friends. Rachel and Emily shared a lot in common, having both attended and graduated from law school. Even though Rachel hadn't taken the bar exam, she was still a lawyer, just not licensed. Eventually the women's lives took different paths; they saw each other less and less. But when they did see one another, it was as if time hadn't passed.

After Rachel died, Emily tried to keep in touch with her daughter Stephanie. It became more difficult to maintain any meaningful contact with her after Brad married Beverly; their relationship became strained to the point of literally having no contact. Stephanie adored her father, and she felt an instant bond to his new wife. Emily had her career and her jobs to keep her busy, and finding time to spend with Stephanie was a chore she didn't look forward to. So instead of trying to maintain a relationship with the young woman, she resorted to an occasional phone call on holidays and birthdays. Other than that, she didn't see her.

Emily had her suspicions about the accident, but Eric convinced her the crash was simply due to pilot error. Now that there had been yet another accident, and this time Stephanie was dead, Emily no longer doubted the first crash wasn't intentional. Brad was a superior pilot. If anyone could fly a plane, crash-land, cause the death of two families, and still survive, it was Brad. He wasn't just any pilot; he had a commercial license and he was a flight instructor. Flying wasn't his hobby; it was a passion—or perhaps even an addiction. Whatever it was, it was in his blood.

...

Brad's flight was uneventful, and he left the airport in a cab and headed straight for home, imagining the quiet and stillness of his house. Once home he went through his desk, looking for the name of the funeral director who had taken care of his first family. Finding Belsky's number, he made arrangements to speak to the funeral director the following morning.

Nineteen

The next morning, Brad drove to the cemetery. He hadn't been there since Rachel and the children's funeral. He wanted to make sure there was space next to Rachel that would hold a few more graves.

He pulled into the cemetery and made his way through the winding paths until he came to the narrow dirt road that led to the graves of his first wife and children. He parked at the end of the road and got out of the car. The dirt road was wet from an early-morning rain, so he reached under the driver's seat and removed plastic shoe covers. He had no intention of getting mud on his shoes. He placed them over his shoes and walked toward the graves.

He stood in front of Rachel's grave, not moving, thinking not of Rachel or their life together but whether there was enough room to place Stephanie next to her mother and whether there was room enough for Beverly and her boys to be placed a respectful distance from Stephanie. He smiled when he realized there was plenty of room and then turned to walk to his car, not once looking back.

...

Seth had been watching Dr. Rivers's house. He knew when Brad had come home the night before, and he watched him leave his house for Tinker's Hill Cemetery. He kept a safe distance behind as he followed him. He knew where Dr. Rivers's first family was buried, and he knew the second family would also be buried in that same cemetery. He parked his car down the hill from where Brad had parked, pretending to be visiting a grave, but his eyes never left Brad. He waited until Brad left before walking up to Rachel's grave. He removed a small dried daisy from the inside of his jacket and carefully placed it on top of her headstone. Then he turned away from her grave and started the short walk to where he had parked his car.

Leaving the cemetery, he followed Brad. He was fairly certain he knew where Brad was going, but he needed to be absolutely certain. When Brad turned and pulled into Belsky's Funeral Home, he had the confirmation he had expected. Brad was using the same funeral director, same funeral home, and same cemetery he had used to bury his first family.

...

During the drive to the funeral home to make the arrangements, Brad thought about the order in which the graves should be placed. He knew Stephanie was going next to her mother—that was a given—but he might have to bury the rest a short distance away from her and her mother. To be honest, he really didn't care where the bodies were buried, or even if there was a funeral. Placing the bodies in one location would simply be easier and more convenient, and after it was over, he knew he wouldn't return. The funeral and burial were simply a formality, something that must be done when someone dies. He would have preferred cremations, but that might have looked too callous, not to mention suspicious.

Brad planned to hold the funerals on a Sunday afternoon. His second wife, Beverly, had been a devout Catholic, and she would have wanted her funeral to be on a Sunday. Even though it was early fall, the weather was still warm during the day, with a nice cool breeze in the afternoon. The leaves had begun changing colors from green to brilliant reds and yellows, but most still clung to their stems, with only a few falling.

Brad picked the perfect location for the graves. As expected, he chose the same cemetery he had used to bury his first wife, their sons, and Stephanie's twin sister. The site was nestled in the back of the cemetery among the trees. He liked how the trees changed from season to season, but mostly he liked that this part of the cemetery was secluded. To reach the graves he had to drive down a narrow dirt road, park literally in the road, and walk several feet up a hill to get to the graves.

He pulled into the driveway of the funeral home, the typical gray stone building with a large circular parking lot in the front and an even larger parking lot in the back. He parked his BMW in the space furthest from the door, in the back lot. He always parked as far away from the doors as possible. He liked his privacy, and besides, walking was good.

His cell phone rang as he approached the front doors. It was Claire. Brad was instantly irritated. He had given her specific instructions not to contact him, and he thought he had made his instructions clear. He needed to focus on the funeral arrangements, and an interruption from a former lover was an unnecessary distraction he neither wanted nor needed. He had a feeling that Claire was expecting their relationship to resume now that his wife was dead. He would need to ensure that she completely understood there would be no resuming their relationship, and he would also ensure that she kept her mouth shut. Ignoring her call, he silenced his phone.

Brad had made the appointment the day before to meet with the funeral director. Since he was trying to come across as a grieving husband and father, he was intentionally late. Brad slowly walked into the foyer of the funeral home and quietly announced to the receptionist that he was there to meet with Mr. Belsky, the funeral director. The receptionist was an older woman, slightly overweight, who wore her hair in a bun on top of her head. She had been pretty once, he thought, but time or genetics was not in her favor. She quickly notified Belsky that his noon appointment had arrived. Brad didn't wait long, as Belsky almost immediately came out of his office.

"Dr. Rivers, I am very sorry for your loss," said Belsky, extending his hand. The funeral director was a short, bald, slightly overweight man with soft hands that squished when Brad shook his hand. Brad had never been impressed with Belsky. He asked too many questions and smiled way too much for a funeral director. He reminded Brad of the Cheshire Cat.

"Thank you, Mr. Belsky. I am stunned that I am here again. But you did such a wonderful job the last time, I knew I could trust you this time as well."

"Of course, we will do the best for your family." Belsky's voice was soft, with a hint of a European accent, and when he spoke, he almost purred the words.

Brad looked around the entrance of the funeral home. "Mr. Belsky, I was wondering if you could make the arrangements for me. Last time I wasn't able to make the decisions, as I was severely injured. I just can't bring myself to do this. It's such a shock. You understand."

"Of course. We just need for you to pick out the caskets, decide on a date for the service, and pick a cemetery. I can make the location arrangements if you want, or you can pick the location," answered Belsky.

Perhaps his accent is German or Austrian, Brad wondered absently. Brad was making a very good effort at avoiding the funeral director's gaze, and although it was rare for him to feel uncomfortable, he was beginning to feel unnerved as he noticed Belsky intently watching his movements. But if Belsky was suspicious, he wasn't giving any indication to Brad.

"I would appreciate that very much," Brad said as he continued to avoid the funeral director's eyes. "Please make all the arrangements as before."

...

Belsky had been carefully watching Brad. He had his suspicions. He had always had his suspicions. In fact, he was certain this time Brad was responsible for the accident. Belsky just didn't know how he'd done it.

Even though he had always thought Brad was probably responsible for the first accident, being responsible for making a mistake was completely different from being responsible for the intentional deaths of his family. And how did he survive two plane crashes? He expected the authorities to ask questions or, at the very least, attend the funeral. It wasn't uncommon for the police or the DA's office to attend a funeral for the sole purpose of watching the crowd to determine if anything was out of the ordinary.

Belsky had his own opinion about what happened, but it wasn't his place to say anything. Whether it was a failed murder-suicide was one for the courts to decide—or for God to decide. Belsky wasn't one to judge; he had seen hundreds of grieving families and spouses. But Brad never looked or acted like he was grieving. He acted as if he were shopping for furniture, and his dark eyes were empty when he spoke. In the end it didn't matter to Belsky, though; Brad was a customer, and money never seemed to be an object for him.

"Mr. Belsky, can you pick the caskets for me? Price is not an issue, and I want a white one for my daughter. Please arrange for the flowers. I don't care what you order. I'm using the same cemetery,

Tinker's Hill. I want Stephanie next to her mother and the rest in the same general area. I just came from the cemetery; there seems to be enough room. Oh, and make the service on a Sunday."

Belsky's thin smile slowly disappeared. He had no doubt Brad had somehow killed both of his families, but he carefully responded to Brad's request. "Of course, we can do all of this. I understand how overwhelmed you must be to lose your wife and children again." He watched for a reaction from Brad, but wasn't surprised to not see one.

"Thank you again, Mr. Belsky," Brad said as he turned for the door. "Please just let me know when the arrangements are made."

Belsky followed after him. "Dr. Rivers, we need you to sign the financial papers and the consents so we can follow your instructions."

Brad stopped and turned around. With a quick smile, he walked back toward the funeral home, replying curtly, "I should think you would have had this ready for me as opposed to making me wait. I am very busy, and this is taking up valuable time." He brushed past Belsky as he walked back into the funeral home.

Fifteen minutes later he walked out again, this time with Belsky watching him from his office window. Belsky wondered why no one suspected Rivers or questioned him about how he had somehow managed to crash a plane twice, walking away with barely any injuries, yet killing his family each time.

The funeral home made all the arrangements, including ordering the flowers and publishing the announcements. And per Dr. Rivers's instructions, the service was set on the following Sunday afternoon. Belsky made several attempts to contact Brad by phone and even by text message, which was against his personal policy and the policy of the funeral home, but he was unable to reach him. *Perhaps the good Dr. Rivers won't show up for his family's funeral*, thought Belsky. But eventually he did receive a text message from Rivers acknowledging receipt of his previous messages.

Twenty

Brad arrived at the funeral home a couple of hours prior to the funeral. His expectations for the service were high when he walked into the viewing room. Beverly was in the first casket. Next to Beverly was Stephanie's white casket, followed by the boys. Each casket was closed, with a large portrait of the deceased in an intricate frame sitting on top. Each of the portraits was nestled in a bed of fresh flowers. Beverly's casket had an array of red roses that extended from the middle of her casket to the end. Stephanie's casket had an equally beautiful array of multicolored flowers, but hers were fresh-cut seasonal blooms with a more youthful flair. Brad was standing back, admiring Belsky's work, when he heard the funeral director approach him from behind.

"Mr. Belsky, I have to admit this is very nicely done. I think my wife would have liked this, and I especially like what you did with

Stephanie's casket."

Belsky cleared his throat. "Thank you, Dr. Rivers. We try to do our best to service our clients' needs, as well as take care of the deceased."

"I know, Mr. Belsky. I was just thinking the guests will be impressed with how lovely this looks. People should start coming very soon."

Belsky nodded in agreement and left Brad in the viewing parlor. He walked back to the front of the funeral home, wondering how many people would actually show up and whether he had enough space in the parlor. Brad expected everything to be perfect. The service was scheduled to start at one p.m. It was almost noon, and cars were just now beginning to arrive.

...

Emily was the first to arrive at the funeral home. She had caught the early flight out of Boston and came straight from the airport directly to the funeral home.

She parked her rental car in the side parking lot but couldn't bring herself to get out of the car. Instead, she sat in the car crying softly, thinking of Stephanie and Rachel. She couldn't help but wonder if Brad had planned to kill his family, and if he did, why? She didn't care how bad she looked when she did get out of the car. She could hear other cars approaching and parking in the lot.

Just as she decided to get out of her car and walk into the funeral home, a black BMW pulled in next to her. She waited until the driver turned off the engine, before getting out at the same time as the other driver. It was Eric. Her breath caught in her throat when she saw him. She hadn't seen him since Rachel's funeral. She instinctively looked away when their eyes met; she wasn't ready to face him. Even though years had passed, she still loved him. She knew she had not only disappointed him, but she had also abandoned him. There were so many things she wanted to say, but she no longer had the words. And she doubted if he would be interested in what she had to say anyway.

"Emily? I'm glad you were able to make it."

Gathering her strength, she looked up at him. He was the same as she had remembered: tall, handsome. Even his wavy hair was the same light-brown color. He walked around the back of his car to where she was standing and took her in his arms. Her eyes were slightly wet with tears; she lowered her head and cried softly on his chest. She didn't have the energy to wipe the tears away, and when she finally looked up into his eyes, they were still soft and loving. She felt herself wishing she had never left Eric, that she hadn't run away from their life together. It wasn't just that he had defended Brad. Eric flew with Brad; they were very close friends, and Eric was his attorney. Hell, they even drove the same type of car. She couldn't help but wonder if Eric was somehow involved. She desperately wanted to believe he wasn't involved with either accident; maybe he was just clueless. And she had to admit the accident wasn't her only reason for leaving. She had needed a new start, and staying with Eric wasn't a new start. She stammered, trying to find words to respond to him as he held her and drew her close.

Through his own tears, Eric told her how sorry he was, how wrong he had been for letting her leave, for not going after her, and for letting her believe he stopped loving her.

"Eric, I know, it's OK. I was wrong too. I am so sorry I left the way I did," she cried. She found the embrace comforting and forced herself to pull away. It was time to walk into the funeral home.

He kept his arm around her as they walked into the service together and joined several other mourners. Eric recognized a few of the attendees as Brad's partners and office staff. The room where the service was held was small, but large enough to seat a few dozen people. Brad was in the front of the room talking with the priest. He didn't seem to pay attention to any of the mourners, if he noticed them at all.

Just as Rachel had been Catholic, so were Beverly and her sons. Brad had attended Mass with Stephanie at St. Mary's parish, but he had never joined. Only Rachel and the children had been members. The church had agreed to hold the service at the funeral home. Following the introductory rite, which included sprinkling of the holy water, came the liturgy of the Word. Beverley's sister and brother did the readings. Traditionally eulogies are given during a vigil or wake instead of during a Catholic Mass, but just as the last strains of the Communion song ended, Brad quickly stood and strode to the lectern to speak. The room had already been quiet, but now all eyes rested on Brad. He cleared his throat and for an instant appeared anxious and uneasy, but he quickly recovered his composure. He spoke of how much he loved Beverly and the children, how much he would miss them, and that he would never be able to replace them.

"After losing Rachel and the children, I thought I would never again find someone to share my life and dreams, someone I could partner with, have children with, and laugh with again," he said. "Beverly and her children brought all that back into my life, my world." Brad spoke softly and slowly, without looking at anyone, pausing for effect. Then, slowly raising his head, he scanned the faces of the mourners, and with teary eyes he sat down behind the podium.

Twenty-One

SETH HAD ARRIVED AT THE FUNERAL HOME AS THE MOURNERS BEGAN ARRIVING. He waited outside in his car, watching the people walk into the building. After the service started, he quietly slipped in and took a seat in the back of the room. He missed the sprinkling of the holy water but arrived in time to hear the opening prayer. He found comfort and solace in Catholic Masses and prayers. He didn't believe in any God, per se, but he supposed there was some kind of higher being. However, if there was truly a God, as the Christians claimed, their God had failed humanity, and he had failed Rachel and her children. And that was in opposition to the Christian faith, wherein followers believe God answers all prayers. Regardless, the service, prayers, and softly sung hymns relaxed him.

He knew the order of a Catholic funeral, and when Dr. Rivers jumped up to speak following the Communion, he was appalled. It didn't matter that he wasn't Catholic or that he really didn't believe in God; he did believe in tradition and following protocol to the letter. The eulogy should come at the vigil before the funeral or possibly at the cemetery. Not here and not now! But still he listened; there was much to learn.

Seth looked over the group. Some he knew, but most he didn't recognize. Sitting in the middle of the room at the end of a row were Eric Wilkerson and Emily Bridges; he recognized them from the news. He was surprised they were sitting together, as he thought they were no longer a couple. Not only were they seated together, they seemed to actually *be* together. *Interesting*, he thought. If it weren't for them, Seth believed this funeral would not be taking place. His research into the plane crashes suggested they each had a part in the deaths. For Eric, his part was less than Emily's, but in his gut Seth was convinced that Eric was just as guilty and just as responsible. In fact, he believed it may have been possible for Eric to have prevented the flight. He wasn't sure how, yet. He would need to be certain before he made any decision concerning Eric. At the moment, his focus was on Dr. Rivers.

Dr. Rivers gave a beautiful speech about how wonderful his wife Beverly had been, how he had been lost following the death of his first wife, Rachel, and that Beverly brought him out of the darkness into the light with her laughter, her love of life, and her children. He couldn't help but notice that he didn't say a word about Stephanie. He glanced over the crowd of mourners to see if any of them had noticed the same, if they had any reaction—even a slight reaction—to Rivers's speech. The mourners, including Eric and Emily, sat stiffly in their seats, some crying, some looking away, but all appearing to have the same reaction and look upon their faces. It wasn't just grief he saw, but shock and disbelief in both their faces and body language, except for one person, a woman who kept looking at Brad. He wondered who she was; she was picking at her nail polish and looked bored with the service.

When the Mass was over, the group slowly got in line to

approach the caskets. Most carried flowers that they placed upon the closed caskets. When they were finished, they left the room, but very few spoke to Dr. Rivers. Some shook his hand, but most avoided eye contact with him. Seth waited until the procession line was almost complete, and then he got behind the last of the mourners and placed a red rose upon each casket. He stopped in front of Stephanie's casket, looking at her picture, and then very gently rested his hand on top of her casket before leaving a rose next to her picture. He continued to Beverly's casket, placed a rose upon hers, and whispered, "I will never forget you." Like the majority of the attendees, he had never personally met Dr. Rivers. The doctor had no idea who he was. But Seth knew who Dr. Rivers was.

When Seth spoke, his voice was even and his words were controlled. "Dr. Rivers, I am so very sorry for your loss."

Rivers shook his hand. "Thank you for coming. How did you know my wife?"

"I didn't," Seth replied.

Brad quickly let go of his hand and gave him a slightly confused look before saying, "Again, thank you for coming. The procession to the cemetery will be leaving soon, but I understand if you can't make it." He glanced around the room as if he were looking for someone. He looked unnerved.

"Of course I will make it, Dr. Rivers," said Seth. "I wouldn't miss it. I suppose you could say our families lived in the same neighborhood when we were children."

He walked away, leaving Brad looking after him. Seth knew he was confused and trying to remember if he had ever met him or which one of his wives had known him.

He also knew Brad was uncomfortable with his presence. Brad's unease and lack of control over who the mourners were gave Seth a slight sense of satisfaction. He followed Rivers's gaze and noticed it had stopped on an attractive woman who appeared to have attended the funeral alone. He noticed she was intently watching Brad, and throughout the service, he caught the couple's quick glances at one another and wondered if anyone else had noticed.

The procession to the cemetery immediately followed the Mass. Only a few close friends and relatives attended the graveside service at the cemetery. Seth, of course, attended. He needed to see, wanted to see, the entire service. He stayed in the back of the crowd, watching each person. Eric and Emily drove together and stood together. Eric kept his arm around Emily's waist, and Emily leaned against him. The woman who appeared interested in Brad also attended the vigil, arriving in the car behind Seth's. She attended alone, and her gaze never left Brad.

Dr. Rivers spoke again. It was obvious Rivers enjoyed listening to himself speak and being the center of attention. As the graveside service ended and the caskets were lowered into the ground, the mourners began to file out and walk back to their cars. Seth waited, watching, and finally saw a glimmer of emotion from the good doctor. After the caskets were each in their respective places and the crowd had left, Rivers turned with a thin smile on his face as the grave diggers began covering the caskets with dirt. Instead of placing flowers on top of the caskets as those in the procession had done, Rivers wiped his hands as if he had dirt on them and then turned and walked away without looking back.

Very few of the mourners spoke to Brad as they left the cemetery. The ones who did didn't have much to say and quickly left. Seth waited until everyone had left the area before calling out to Brad, who was walking back down the path toward his car. Brad glanced over at the sound of his name and saw Seth. He shouted back, not hiding his irritation. "If you didn't know my wife, why are you here? I don't even know your name. Is there anything else you need? Or is there something you want?"

Brad stopped walking toward the cars and instead waited as he watched Seth make his way back up the hill. Seth purposefully walked slowly, making Brad wait. Brad made no attempt to meet him halfway. Perhaps he thought he was a reporter or a detective.

Seth stopped a few feet away from Brad and carefully began to speak. "Brad, this may not be the right time to ask questions or ask a favor of a friend, but I was wondering if you still had the charter service? I have some business to attend to out of state, and I would prefer to get in and out on my time and not wait on an airline."

"Yeah, of course I do. You can call Krannert to schedule a flight if you need to, but at the moment, I am obviously not flying. And we are not friends. In fact, I have never seen you, and I have absolutely no idea who you are." Brad's response was short and icy.

"Of course. I knew you weren't flying. My concern was whether Krannert's Charter was still operational or not."

"It is, and I have other pilots who are able to fly. I am not the only pilot. With a busy medical practice, I don't have time to fly charters for clients. I only fly for myself and my family." Brad's eyes never left Seth's face while he spoke.

"Your family?" Seth scoffed. "You won't be flying for your family anymore. You saw to that. But tell me, Dr. Rivers, how did you manage to survive?"

Without waiting for an answer, Seth turned and made his way back down the hill toward his car. He could feel Brad's glare on his back, but he didn't care. He didn't have an actual business that required a charter flight. His rationale for asking Brad about Krannert and the charter business was to see if he was planning to fly again and whether Brad would be at the airstrip. Just one question, and Brad had given him all the answers he needed.

There were many ways to punish a guilty person. Jury trial, conviction, and sentencing were just one. He knew of many other more effective methods that satisfied the primal need of some humans.

He opened his car door, slowly sat in the driver's seat, and watched while Brad drove away from the cemetery. He wasn't ready to leave, though. He couldn't leave. He sat in the car, remembering.

Twenty-Two

In the summer of 1984, the house next to his family's had finally sold, and the new family was moving in. He stood in the library window watching the movers unload the furniture. The house next door was a small bungalow. The driveways of the two homes were next to each other, with a narrow hedge separating them. He couldn't wait to see who was moving next door. He had hoped there would be kids and that they wouldn't be too young. He was ten, and most of the neighborhood kids were little and couldn't even ride a bike.

A blue Oldsmobile slowly pulled into the driveway. Holding his breath, he waited to see who would open the door. *Please, God, don't let it be another old couple*, he thought.

A man and a woman got out of the front seat. They looked to be about as old as his parents. *That's good*, he thought. *It's a start.* He could see movement in the back seat. He didn't care if they had a boy or a girl, just as long as the kid was his age and not in diapers!

Finally the rear driver's-side door opened. "Come on, get out!" he shouted softly to no one. He pressed his face against the window pane and saw red sneakers with white ankle socks. *Humph, must be a girl*, he thought. He was disappointed, but maybe she would be OK.

"Rachel!" called her father. "Get out of the car!"

"OK, I am!" she shouted back. "Just hang on."

Finally he saw her crawl out of the car. *Not too bad*, he thought. She looked to be his age. She had light-brown hair, pulled up into a ponytail. As she got out of the car, she glanced at the monstrous house sitting next to her small house and saw him peering down at her. He quickly sank back from the window, but he knew it was too late. She had seen him.

He waited a few minutes, gathered up his courage, and made his way out of his house and to her driveway. As he walked around the hedgerow that separated their two yards, onto her driveway, he practiced how he would introduce himself. But by the time he rounded the hedge, Rachel and her father were no longer next to the car. Gathering his courage he walked up the sidewalk toward the front door. He raised his fist to knock on the door just as it opened and Rachel ran out, almost running him over.

"Uh, hello," she said.

"Yeah, hi, I live there, next door," he said, pointing to his house.

"Yeah, I know, I saw you. I'm Rachel. Your house is huge and kinda creepy. But I like it."

"It's just big; nothing creepy about it. I can show you around if my parents say it's OK," he said.

They spent the rest of the afternoon talking and laughing as he helped her unpack her room. They finished just as it was getting dark. Afterward they sat on the front porch steps; her mom brought sandwiches and sweet tea for them. He couldn't remember a happier time.

That summer went by fast. It was the first summer he remembered that he hadn't been lonely. Finally he had someone to play with and share his secrets with. Not all of his secrets, of course. And he was worried that when school started Rachel would make new friends and forget about him, becoming someone who whispered behind his back. But that never happened. Instead, the two became almost inseparable. They walked to and from school together, did their homework together, and sometimes ate dinner and watched evening television together. When winter finally came, they played in the snow.

"Come on, lie down in the snow!" Rachel said, giggling, as she tossed herself backward into the newly fallen snow. "Do you know what a snow angel is?"

He shook his head no.

"Just watch me make one and then you can make one. The trick is getting out of the snow without ruining the angel."

Rachel dropped down onto the snow, raised and lowered her arms, and moved her legs across the snow to make the wings and the gown of the angel. When she was satisfied with her art, she carefully got up and climbed out of the angel shape. He was still admiring her work when she said, "Your turn," and gently pushed him toward the snow-covered yard.

Laughing, he fell on the snow-covered grass. "OK, OK. I'm gonna do it, just lookin' for the right spot."

He hurriedly made his snow angel and jumped out instead of carefully getting up. The bottom of the angel looked a little ragged. Although it was dark, it was also bright enough outside to see the snow falling. The air was crisp and clean. It wasn't too cold, and there was no wind. The night was quiet, and all he remembered years later was hearing the snow falling onto the ground.

"Well, that's an awfully nice snow angel for being your first," Rachel said. She laughed and threw her arms around his shoulders. Together they stood there admiring their snow angels as the snow continued to fall. He would always remember that night as the happiest night of his childhood.

Twenty-Three

Sitting in his car, looking up the hill to where Rachel and her children were buried, Seth felt an intense sadness and loss as he remembered the first day he met Rachel. That evening, sitting on the porch eating bologna sandwiches and drinking sweet tea, was the beginning of a lifelong friendship he treasured. He missed her terribly. And now that Stephanie was gone, there was nothing left of Rachel.

Pushing the ignition button and picking up his cell, he called Brad while still looking up at the graves. After several rings, Brad answered. He could hear the irritation in his voice as he muttered hello.

He had never met Brad before the funeral. Rachel had known early on that if Brad was aware of Seth, he would have forced Rachel to give up his friendship. He was one, if not the only, secret Rachel had kept from Brad. Seth knew Brad wasn't always the wonderful, loving husband Rachel had made him out to be, but she never knew that, even though Seth kept his agreement to keep his and Rachel's friendship in the shadows, he also kept careful watch on the doctor. He knew more about Brad than anyone, including Rachel, could ever imagine.

"Brad, I was thinking we should get together and talk. I think it's time you get to know me."

Brad took a few seconds to reply before realizing who the caller was. "Look, I have no idea who you are or how you got my personal number. I have no idea what you want, nor do I care. Don't call me again. If you do, you won't like the outcome." He hung up without saying goodbye or waiting for a response.

Seth slowly moved the cell away from his ear and placed it in the cup holder in the center console of his car. He knew what he was going to do, what he had to do. The anticipation and preparation were just part of the game. But carrying out the plan—that was where the excitement was, and he couldn't wait to feel that rush when the shine went out of the eyes of his kills. He was grateful he had kept his promise to Rachel. There would be no connection between himself and the good doctor. But with this kill, unlike all the others before, he would make certain his victim knew exactly why he was about to die.

Twenty-Four

Immediately following the funerals, Brad drove straight to Krannert. Given that it was a Sunday, the hangars would be empty, with the possible exception of weekend private pilots who only flew recreationally. He parked and quickly walked into his office. The calls from whoever that guy was had unnerved him. He said he didn't know his wife. Was he lying, did he know Beverly? Brad knew all of Beverly's friends and close family. He even knew of her past boyfriends. Before they married, he had ordered a background check on her. There wasn't anything about her he didn't know. So who was this guy, why did he show up at the funerals, and what did he know, if anything?

He needed to touch base with Eric and Tedesco. He had an idea who the guy at the cemetery was, but he wasn't certain. He would need to have Eric look into it, and if Eric wasn't able to help, then he would hire someone to find out who he was and what he wanted. Brad knew Tedesco was watching, and he wondered if this guy was one of his men. Maybe this guy thought he knew something and was going to try to blackmail him.

Brad set about calling Eric first. He answered on the first ring.

"Hey, we need to discuss Tedesco. I have a few messages from him. There has to be a charter in the next few weeks. You have to clear your schedule."

"Really, Brad? Given the circumstances, I am the only one who can fly for him. You took care of that without consulting me. So, you do what I say, and this time you will listen to me."

Eric was livid; he didn't like to be told what to do. He and Brad were equal partners, and Brad knew Eric couldn't just change his schedule. If he had court appearances, he would either need to get opposing counsel to agree to a continuance, or he would have to file for one and attend a hearing and wait for the judge to decide. "You call him, and you call him now. Find out when he wants the next charter. And, Brad, you better hope to God I can make the date." Eric hung up on him. Deep down he knew they would make the charter, and he also knew he would get past his anger.

Brad's next call was to the monsignor. "Monsignor Tedesco, are you available to talk?"

"Dr. Rivers, I was expecting a call from you. May I offer my condolences?" The sarcasm in the monsignor's voice did not go unnoticed.

"Yes, thank you, Monsignor," Brad said stiffly. "I called to discuss the next charter. Eric told me you needed to arrange a charter in the next few weeks. I am not able to fly, but I will be there with Eric to help with the shipment."

Over the past several years, Brad and Eric had supplemented their incomes by providing a discreet charter service to the monsignor and his associates. Fortunately, the charter service was only needed once or twice a year, and they were able to make quick stops in and out of Italy. The three men had formed a unique business arrangement.

Whenever the monsignor needed a private flight, they assisted. In fact, this side business had kept Krannert afloat in the early days of the airstrip. Of course, the money was kept in offshore accounts and occasionally transferred in small amounts to a Bank of America branch. Then, several months later, the money would be deposited as a business investment to Krannert's Airport to be used for improvements, salaries, and bonuses. Both Eric and Brad were very careful to only transfer funds every few months, and only in amounts less than ten thousand dollars. Occasionally, one of them would make a vacation trip to the Caymans to withdraw cash. Brad had his funds transferred to not only himself but his wife's account as well. Neither Rachel nor Beverly knew about the accounts. Even after Rachel died, Brad kept her account open, and he fully intended to keep Beverly's open too.

"Dr. Rivers, yes, we will be requiring your service in the coming weeks. This charter will most likely be the last one of this type. I hope we can get this arranged and completed in the next few weeks. I will be in touch."

Sighing, Tedesco leaned back in his leather chair and placed the phone in its receiver on his desk. He had first met Brad purely by accident when he and his first wife, Rachel, visited Vatican City. He had once thought they were what God would have wanted a married couple to be. Brad was attentive and caring; he seemed to strive to make Rachel happy. Rachel genuinely appeared to have loved her husband. The trip was a surprise gift for her birthday. He couldn't remember how old she was turning, just that the trip was one of a lifetime. She had always dreamed of seeing the Vatican and of attending a Mass said by the pope. For this gift to his wife, Brad hadn't left anything to chance and had contacted a local travel agency in Italy. It was through this travel agency that Tedesco had learned about Brad and his charter service.

After learning of Brad's request to take his wife to the Vatican, Tedesco had made the arrangements himself for Brad and Rachel to stay inside Vatican City, which was almost impossible for a noncitizen. Tedesco also offered his own home for their use.

A knock on his office door brought Tedesco back to the present. "It's open," he called out.

"Monsignor, I was instructed by the secretary to the cardinals to give you this invitation and to wait for your response," said the papacy courier.

Tedesco took the invitation and opened it gently. The envelope was the traditional scarlet red with gold embossed letters. The calligraphy on the envelope was a work of art. The invitation and RSVP card were also handwritten in the same style. The invite was more of a polite demand for his participation in an audit meeting rather than an invite. He filled out the RSVP and handed it back to the courier. "Please take this back to the secretary and tell him that I will, of course, attend."

Twenty-Five

Founded in the mid-1900s, the Institute for the Historical Safekeeping of Christianity—often referred to as the Institute—was a private financial institution located inside Vatican City. The Vatican used the Institute to safeguard artwork and cultural pieces during times of conflict. Once the conflict was over, the works of art, money, and other items that had been collected were returned to the owners. Over the years, the Institute grew into a fully operational bank capable of maintaining and managing the Vatican's wealth. The bank's vaults contained countless works of art given to it for safekeeping during the German occupation, as well as rumored millions in Nazi gold, and its own separate funds. Only Church officials and members of the Vatican and their families were allowed to make deposits into the bank. The bank's deposits, investments, and expenses, as well as the guardianship of properties, were overseen by five cardinals who reported directly to the Vatican's secretary of state, who, in turn, reported solely to the pope. But the pope was not involved in the day-to-day activities of the bank; that was left to the five cardinals. The cardinals appointed the president, whose term was a lifetime appointment. Every president since the inception of the bank had been either a cardinal or a monsignor of the Vatican. The five cardinals also appointed the bank's accountant, and his appointment was also a lifetime appointment. By keeping the bank's employees and administrators members of the Vatican, the bank was able to maintain its secrecy and much-needed protection for the various treasures it held.

Monsignor Tedesco was appointed as the bank's accountant almost two decades ago. He had been well into his thirties when he was called to the priesthood. Prior to becoming a priest he had been the chief accountant for the National Bank of Italy, and was well known for his precision and expertise. He had already amassed a sizable wealth when he was called to join the priesthood. With his background, after completing seminary and being ordained, the Vatican quickly placed him as an accountant for the Vatican Bank. Over the years, he advanced from overseeing routine deposits to auditing and maintaining accurate records of the rumored Nazi gold and other protected property being safeguarded by the bank.

Tedesco couldn't have found a better position within the Vatican at which to work. He reported only to the president of the bank. He was also responsible for performing annual audits and maintaining the inventory of the protected art, gold, and property. With his position he had access to the archives and libraries of the Vatican. Along with having a talent with numbers, he was fluent in ancient Italian and Latin. The records in the vaults were written mostly in Italian, but some were in Latin. Within the Latin documents, there was information that contained the location of a vault the Vatican had forgotten. It was this vault that eventually created the need for Krannert's Charter Service.

Tedesco didn't realize at first that the vault had been forgotten. It wasn't until he completed a long-overdue audit that he discovered this vault hadn't been listed in previous years as an asset or a location of protected artifacts. He found the information purely by accident when he compared his current audit with an audit completed in the late 1940s. At first he dismissed it as a mistake or a vault that had once existed but did not any longer. It wasn't until he had been sent to Denmark for a conference almost fifteen years ago that he decided to check out whether the vault still existed.

...

Nykøbing Mors, Denmark, was an old city once used as a shipyard. According to the Vatican archives, the vault Tedesco was looking for was inside one of its old churches. The church was built in the late 1600s of orange-red brick with a slate roof. The windows were narrow but contained beautiful stained glass. The tops of the windows were arched. The church rested on a hilltop, and the grounds were surrounded by wrought-iron fences. Over the years, the church had been renovated and modernized, and to this day it was still fully functional. It had two basements. The elevator only went to the first-level basement. According to the archives, the vault, if it remained, was hidden inside the second-level basement, which was only accessible by a hidden staircase behind a wall-to-wall German *schrank*. The only document Tedesco had been able to find was an old postcard with a picture of the church on one side and the address on the other.

He arrived at the church late in the day. It was autumn, and the trees were brilliant shades of red, yellow, and orange. He pulled up to the gate, leaned out the window, and pushed the buzzer. Immediately a female voice asked, "Hej, kan jeg hjaelpe dig?"

Tedesco replied, "Taler du Engelsk?"

The voice laughed. "Monsignor Tedesco, drive slowly, the gate will open."

The iron gate swung open, and he entered the grounds of the church. It was still just as majestic as it had been in its prime. *The war missed this one*, he said to himself.

An older woman dressed in a traditional nun's habit met him at the door and eagerly led him into the foyer. As he entered, he stopped and dipped his index finger into the font of the holy water, making the sign of the cross before stepping into the body of the church. He looked around the church, admiring the stained-glass windows, the heavy wooden benches, and the raised altar. He had always found the older churches to be the most beautiful. Bowing slightly to the nun, he asked, "May I have the honor of knowing your name?"

Her accent was light, and he wasn't sure if she was Danish.

"You can call me Sister Maria, Monsignor. Let me show you the church, and then we can go to Father Joseph's office."

Sister Maria gave him a quick tour of the church before leading him to the office of the priest. She gently knocked on the door, and not waiting for a response, she opened it. Father Joseph was an elderly priest with snow-white hair and round glasses. He was standing by a bookcase that Tedesco imagined was the entrance to the basement. The elder priest walked up to Tedesco and embraced him, kissing him on each cheek.

"So, you are here to see the basement. I won't be going down with you. My knees have seen better days, and no one at my age needs a broken hip."

Father Joseph walked back toward his desk, waving his hand at the bookcases. "I haven't been in that basement for the better part of twenty years, Tedesco. Never had a reason to go down there. I think looters over the years took whatever of value was once there. The Vatican stopped taking inventory decades ago. I know I am getting up there in years, but I don't recall ever seeing anything down there except dirt."

"Father Joseph, that's OK. As head of accounting for the Vatican, I do have an obligation to check all the secured locations of valuables that we have recorded. This church is listed as one of those locations.

If there is nothing in the basement, then I will close this and no one will need to come back. If there is property, I will inventory it, ensure it is properly preserved, and the Vatican will continue to safeguard it." Tedesco turned toward the bookcase as if waiting for the mystery door to open.

Father Joseph chuckled "Ah, Monsignor, the door isn't in the bookcase. Everyone knows to look for a hidden door in a bookcase."

The wall behind the bookcase was constructed of irregularly shaped stones. The old priest ran his hand along the wall next to the bookcase. The secret door was not what he expected. The door was part of the stone wall. It wasn't smooth or even; it was just as irregular in shape as the stones it was recessed in.

"It isn't what you expected, Monsignor," said the elder priest. Taking a deep breath, the older priest continued to speak. "You know, back in the war, there were secret rooms everywhere. Rooms to hide people, rooms to hide things. Secret doors couldn't be in places one would immediately find. The church is built on what appears to be two sections of the same basement. To some it would appear to be two separate basements, but in reality there is only one basement with two entrances. The wall separating the two parts of the basement is very thick. I no longer remember how thick it is or how to open the second door. I do know that the part where the church kept the art and property is under what is now the parking lot. It wouldn't have taken the Nazis long to find a fake bookcase that led to a room or a basement. The church was very careful. Not only did we protect the property of the people, we hid the people too. And when the people left, their property left. I think you have wasted your time."

The priest looked worn; he took a couple of steps back to his chair and gingerly sat down. Watching Tedesco, he continued, "When you get into the basement and look around, you may find something, and then again, you may find nothing."

Tedesco walked to the doorway of the staircase. There was no light to see the stairs. "Father Joseph, do you have a light?" The elderly priest gestured toward the bookcase without speaking. Tedesco followed his gesture and saw a flashlight sitting on a shelf. He reached over to pick up the flashlight and was surprised when it actually worked. He looked again at the priest; Joseph was either snoozing or simply had his eyes closed. Softly, he said, "Thank you, Father."

The basement wasn't as large as he thought it should have been. The floors were dirt, the walls were stone, and the ceiling had wood planks. It wasn't possible for the Vatican to store or protect any type of art in this basement. As he glanced around, he couldn't imagine hiding people in this small, dark hole. He pulled the audit record out of his inner jacket pocket. According to the record, the basement should be larger. Perhaps he was in the wrong church. This simply didn't make sense. Everything with the church followed the Vatican's documentation, except this basement.

He took the flashlight and bathed the stone walls in light, looking closely at the stones. He was almost ready to leave the basement when he finally saw it: the symbol of Archangel Michael. At first glance, it looked like a scratch in the wall, but standing back a little, he saw it was obviously an organized stick symbol of the Angel of Strength and Protection.

"Michael," he said under his breath. He ran his hand over the stone and thought it gave a little. He wondered if this was the opening to where the rumored art and gold were kept. He pressed it again, but nothing happened. He felt around the stone, and still nothing. The symbol had a circle on the far left end, a total of three points and one long downward line. "Of course," he muttered. It wasn't the stone with the symbol, but the stone where the line stopped. That stone was flat, almost square in shape, and slightly recessed into the wall. Tedesco felt the stone and ran his hand around the edges. When he did, he heard a click. The wall ever so slightly moved.

He stood back in amazement. There wasn't one secret basement or room; there were two. He pushed open the wall, shone the light into the room, and saw what he had only dreamed of—the Nazi gold. Stacks of gold bars, stacks of dusty bags that had to contain more gold, and small-to-very-large items wrapped in dusty, brittle-looking paper.

Tedesco completed a quick inventory check of the contents of the room. Before leaving the room he picked up one small, dusty bag and placed it in the inner pocket of his jacket. He closed the door as quietly as he could and walked back up the stairs.

"Did you find anything in that room?" asked Father Joseph without looking up.

"Yes, actually, I did find a few items. Not much, though. You were right: there isn't anything in either of the known rooms." Tedesco looked at the elder priest. Father Joseph was leaning back in his leather chair, his arms folded comfortably in his lap with his eyes closed. "I carefully examined the walls and found a small switch that led to another room. I will need to make annual audits. Even though there are only a few items, the Vatican is insistent on maintaining security. Thank you for allowing me access to the basement."

Father Joseph nodded his head in response. Tedesco wasn't sure why he had lied to the priest, and he wasn't even certain if Father Joseph had believed him. He was still trying to comprehend the vastness of his discovery. He also knew that his primary function for the Vatican was to maintain the secrecy of the vault and to protect its contents. He rationalized to himself that was the reason he had lied.

Outside the church and inside the privacy of his car, Tedesco removed the small bag from the inner pocket of his jacket. He gently and carefully opened the cloth bag and peered inside. Once again, he was stunned by the contents. The bag was a least half full of what looked like gold coins. He took one of the coins out of the bag and saw the proof that this was no doubt the rumored Nazi gold. The city name "BERLIN" was stamped along the bottom of the coin, and "DEUTSCHE REICHSBANK" was stamped along the top of the coin. The letters were so small they were barely legible. In the center of each coin, on each side, was the symbol of the Nazis, an eagle atop a swastika with the number 5 to the left of the eagle. The coin was dated 1939.

Tedesco could barely breathe. He sat in shock as he realized his find. He rubbed his thumb over the coin, and turning it over, he rubbed it again. "What are you worth?" he asked quietly. He would count the coins when he returned to his hotel. In the meantime, he placed the coins back into the bag and put the bag back into his jacket pocket.

The drive back to Nykøbing Mors took what seemed like a very long time. Tedesco couldn't stop thinking of the basement, with its stacks of gold bars and bags of gold coins, and wondering what was wrapped in the paper. He felt the bag through his jacket and estimated he had around fifty coins. By the time he made it back to his hotel, he was already thinking of a way to remove the contents of the basement.

It was during this drive that he thought of a pilot who would fly anything for the right amount of money, and this was the initiation of the charter business between Tedesco, Brad, and Eric.

Twenty-Six

Now, fifteen years after the discovery of the vault, Tedesco was being called to a meeting requesting a formal audit. The meeting was to be held in the large conference room at Domus Sanctae Marthae, the official Vatican guesthouse. When Tedesco arrived, he was greeted by the cardinals' secretary, Mr. Castillo, who took his coat and led him into the conference room. All five cardinals were already seated, talking to each other and looking over stacks of paper, as Tedesco took his seat to the right of the fifth cardinal. On the table in front of him was a file. He opened it, and inside was a copy of a letter addressed to the pope by the heads of state for Poland, Hungry, Romania, and Prague on behalf of the Czech Republic. Before he could read the letter, a horn sounded announcing the entrance of the pope. All stood as the pope entered the room.

The pope gestured for everyone to sit after he took his place at the front of the podium. "Good morning, everyone. I am glad you were all able to come at such short notice. In front of each of you is a file that contains a letter by several countries, requesting repatriation of any and all art, property, and gold taken from them and secured by the Vatican during Hitler's regime. The Church has always sought to return all property that was secured during the war to the rightful owners. Several years ago we requested Monsignor Tedesco to audit each of the locations where the Church had stored property on behalf of these countries and people. I have asked all of you to come today so we can discuss completing the repatriation of whatever is left. In past years the Church has always believed the gold was nothing more than a rumor. However, in recent days it has come to the attention of the Institute that there could be some truth to those rumors. According to our head accountant, Monsignor Tedesco, we still have secure locations that contain works of art, property, and even possibly gold."

Cardinal James, one of the only American cardinals at the Vatican, stood to address the pope. "Holy Father, I agree with returning all of what was held for safekeeping, but I am confused, as I thought everything had been returned decades ago. Even if some items were not returned, how do we determine their rightful owners?"

The pope gestured toward Tedesco. "Would you like to address the cardinals, Monsignor?"

Tedesco stood up to address the group. "When I first became the Vatican accountant several years ago, I did an audit of a few—if you will—'safe locations' around northern Europe. It was during this audit that I did, in fact, find art and property, as well as what appeared to be gold bars and coins. As of today, all remains secure and has not been moved or touched in decades."

The cardinals sat quietly, soaking in the information. Tedesco continued to speak. "The problem with returning the property is that we have no way of knowing who the proper owners are anymore. The owners of personal property and art should be easier to determine, but the gold bars and coins will be more difficult. And given the length of time that has passed, it's very possible the owners are no long alive. The question now becomes: To whom do we entrust this property and money?"

The Holy Father arose from his seat. He was visibly angry but understood the accountant's concern. "I want the property and gold inventoried, and the Institute will return to the countries everything it has safeguarded. It is not our place, and has never been our purpose, to find and locate each and every person who had property and money stolen from them! We know the destruction—the world knows the destruction that occurred under the Nazi occupation. The Vatican will entrust the repatriation to the countries, and they will determine how it is to be given back to the people. We cannot continue to hold it for safekeeping, seventy years after it was taken, for it now looks as if the Vatican is profiting from the pain of others! I am ordering an immediate inventory of each secure location, and once we have the inventories, we will invite a representative from each country to the Vatican. We will provide a list of the inventories to each country, and once it is decided how to divide the property and gold, we will arrange transportation for the items to be delivered to each country. In the meantime, I want all the contents of each location delivered to the Institute!"

Tedesco stood to address the pope. "Holy Father, do you have a specific time frame in mind for this? There is a total of five secure locations; each one is several hundred miles apart. Some are in rather remote areas and can only be reached by driving."

"I would like the audit completed before the start of the new year. Once it is complete we will reconvene to decide how best to move forward with contacting the countries. I will compose a letter in response to the request for repatriation, informing them of today's decision and assuring an outcome that will satisfy their request." The Holy Father did not wait for any questions and quickly left the conference room. For a brief moment the cardinals were quiet, and then all at once started asking Tedesco questions.

Once the meeting was over, Tedesco made his way back to his office. He needed to call Brad, but this call would require absolute privacy. His office was not the place to make this call. He finished with the day's work, walked to his home, and checked to ensure his house staff had left for the day. Once his privacy was assured, he called Brad.

Since his initial discovery of the gold under the church in Nykøbing Mors, he had been slowly removing the gold and other treasures. He had hired Brad, and eventually Eric, to fly the gold out of Europe and into the United States, and then to the Caymans. He had never turned in an accurate inventory of the contents of any of the locations. This next delivery would be the last.

Twenty-Seven

"What are you doing here?" Brad said. "Last we spoke, I made myself clear that I wasn't interested in hearing from you. What the hell do you want?"

Brad was instantly pissed and slightly uneasy. He was in the hangar behind the plane when his wife's friend from the funeral surprised him. This guy wasn't very tall, maybe five feet ten inches, but he was muscular. He had short, curly dark-brown hair and piercing dark eyes. He looked familiar, and not just from the funeral.

"Since you have barged into my hangar, I have a question for you. How do you know Beverly? I knew everything about her, and whoever you are, she didn't know you."

The other man didn't reply at first, but just stared at Brad. Then he asked, "What makes you think I knew Beverly?"

Brad took a step closer to him. "Look here, don't play games with me. You came to the funerals, and you told me you knew my wife."

"Yes, and I did know your wife. That was accurate. But I never met Beverly. What I didn't say was that I knew your *first* wife."

He waited for a response and was pleased when he saw a glimmer of nervousness.

"Rachel, it was Rachel I knew. Like I said at the funeral, you could say our families were friends. Let me introduce myself to you. I'm Seth. I knew Rachel many years ago. We were best friends throughout much of our childhood. In fact, we remained friends after she married you. Elizabeth and Stephanie weren't your daughters, Brad; they were mine."

Watching Brad process the information was oddly satisfying.

"The twins were mine. We decided long ago to allow you to believe the girls were yours. We made that decision because we thought it was best for everyone, especially for our daughters. You see, I have a hobby of sorts that doesn't make for a good family life for one child, much less two. And there is always the risk of getting caught. We didn't want them to grow up with that stigma."

"Wait," Brad stammered. "Elizabeth and Stephanie weren't mine?"

"You look surprised, Brad. You don't know as much as you thought you did. Rachel wasn't the demur, submissive housewife you thought she was. I knew the first accident wasn't really an accident, but as long as Stephanie was alive, you would live. Your lifestyle would remain the same, and I would watch and wait."

Brad took a step back and shouted at Seth, "Get out of here before I call the police. You don't come onto my property and threaten me. Get out of my hangar!" He noticed now that Seth's hands were no longer in his pockets and he was smiling. "Listen, you need to leave. Just go!"

"No, Brad, I am not leaving," Seth said as he slowly walked toward Brad, stopping only a few feet in front of him. "I have questions, Brad, and I already know the answers. But I want to hear you say it, and I want to know why."

Before Brad could respond, he felt an instant, sharp, burning pain that began in his chest. Just before he passed out, he realized Seth had shot him with a Taser.

Brad woke up seated in the pilot's seat of his latest jewel, a Piper 341A. He tried to move but was unable. He looked down and saw that he was strapped into the seat; his arms were fastened to his sides with duct tape. Slowly realizing what was happening, he turned to his right and saw Seth sitting in the copilot's seat. Angrily, he shouted, "What the hell do you think you are doing? You get this shit off me and get out of here!"

Seth had been looking out the copilot's window, but now he turned to look at Brad. He waited until Brad was calmer and then said, "Brad, I am not leaving yet. I will when we are finished. Right now we are going to have a chat. You are going to answer my questions, and depending on those answers, I may let you live to see the sun go down. Otherwise, Brad, I am going to kill you."

Brad struggled against the duct tape, still unable to move. "What the hell is wrong with you?" he yelled. "Do you honestly think I am going to do anything you want or tell you anything, you fucked-up piece of shit?"

Seth didn't react to Brad's outburst. Instead he again waited until Brad calmed down and then patiently asked, "Why did you kill Rachel? This is the first question, Brad, and you will answer each and every one of my questions. Don't forget I already know the answers, so if you lie, I am going to know."

"I didn't kill Rachel!" Brad quickly answered. "It was an accident! A horrible accident. You know that. You said you know the answers, so you know the FAA ruled it was an accident."

Seth opened what looked like an old, green steel coffee thermos and poured some of the contents into the cap. He held the cap under Brad's nose.

"Get that shit away from me! Are you crazy?" Brad was nervous now, verging on fear. Surely this guy was bluffing.

Seth smiled and turned in the seat to face Brad. "You killed her and the kids, and it was intentional. Just like this last crash. We both know it was intentional. What I don't know is why you did it. Let me explain how this is going to go down. I am going to ask you a question. For each question you refuse to answer truthfully, I am going to pour a capful of gasoline on whatever part of your body I want to watch burn. But don't worry, you won't burn to death. I will extinguish the fire, and then we will start over again with another question. You will either answer all of the questions, or you will slowly watch yourself burn." Seth waited for Brad to respond. He had no intention of waiting long.

"Seth, is it? Let me reason with you . . . ," Brad stammered.

"Wrong answer, Brad," Seth said as he poured a small capful of the gas onto Brad's upper right thigh and lit a match. Just as he was going to place the burning match on top of his thigh, Brad yelled for him to stop.

"Yes, yes, OK! I killed her! I had to! Damn, I didn't want to. I swear to God, that's the truth. I loved her. I always loved her! I didn't have a choice. She found out about a client in Rome that Eric and I flew charters for occasionally." Brad hung his head and cried softly while trying to determine whether Seth would really burn him alive.

"Were those charters out of Rome? Don't lie to me, Brad."

With a nervous laugh, Brad explained, "No, Eric and I fly charters for a priest out of Vatican City. The actual flights are flown out of Germany, Denmark, or Italy, never directly in or out of the Vatican."

Brad paused until Seth lit another match, then started talking again, faster this time. "The charters were carrying gold, OK? Sometimes art, but mostly gold. We had to get it out of the country and into an offshore bank."

"Whose gold is it, Brad?" Seth asked as he dropped the lit match on Brad's upper right thigh. Brad screamed and fought against the duct tape.

Through his screams he managed to yell, "It was gold collected by—I don't know—various people, and hidden during the Second World War. I am answering your questions, you fucking freak!"

Seth extinguished the fire on Brad's leg with a jacket he had taken from the back seat of the cabin. "Yes, you did answer my question, but you took too long. I am not here to play games. I told you how this was going to go down. You either follow my rules, or I burn you one section at a time."

Brad took a chance and looked over at Seth, who was holding the jacket in one hand and the thermos of gas in his other hand. Seth was looking out the window instead of at Brad. He didn't seem to be paying attention to him. Brad squirmed and pressed against the tape, trying to loosen or even break part of the restraints. "I am trying," Brad said carefully.

Seth nodded his head and turned again to face him. "That's good, Brad, a good start. Now try telling me the details. Who collected the gold, who hid the gold, and how did you become part of the gold trade?" Seth poured another capful of gasoline while waiting for Brad to answer.

Brad slowly drew in a deep breath, trying to calm himself before answering. "I don't know who originally collected the gold. It's rumored that maybe it is Nazi gold, but that was never proven. One of the vaults had been long forgotten." Brad paused again and looked at Seth.

"Go on, Brad. Don't stop."

"OK, OK, just stay calm. I am answering your questions. I met this priest when Rachel and I went to the Vatican. He offered me a job—or opportunity, so to speak. Once the gold was sold, melted, and reformed, it would need to be transported out of Europe. He needed someone to fly it, convert it to cash, and then deposit the cash into various accounts. Eric and I would be paid twenty percent of the profits."

"How much, Brad? How much money over the years did you

get paid? How did Rachel find out?" Seth was still looking out the window, but he was fully aware Brad was trying to get out of the restraints.

"I don't know the exact amount, maybe a little over a million each. I have no idea how Rachel found out. All I know is that I overheard her talking to Emily about the charters. She was upset and threatening to report us." As he talked, Brad was carefully scanning the hangar, looking for anyone he could call out to for help.

"No need to look for help, Brad, it isn't coming. I locked the gate into the airstrip, and it's Sunday; none of your members have flights scheduled. What happened with the phone call between Rachel and Emily?" Seth slowly poured the capful of gas onto Brad's groin and waited for him to speak again.

"You're nuts, you know that? I answered your damn questions!" Brad felt himself losing control and truly feared Seth would light another match.

Seth poured another capful of gas and held it to Brad's chest. "Is this why you killed her and the kids, to keep the charters secret and to save yourself and Eric? And yes, you answered my questions, but you lied to me. You know how Rachel discovered what was going on in Italy. You also know who the gold belongs to. Remember, Brad, I already know the answers. Rachel told me."

Brad's arrogant cockiness was now slipping away as he felt more gas being poured onto his chest. He was trying to remain in control, not that he had any as he was strapped to the pilot's seat.

"Seth," he said, trying to calmly speak in the hope he could reason with the other man. "We both know you aren't going to kill me. OK, you win, you have my attention. Cut the duct tape, let me go, and this will remain between the two of us. I won't talk to anyone about this."

Ignoring Brad's pleas, Seth continued with his questions. "Why were Beverly and Stephanie killed? I know it wasn't an accident." Seth poured another capful of gas, watching Brad and patiently waiting for an answer.

Brad was no longer calm. He was shaking uncontrollably, and his voice quivered when he spoke. "Because I didn't want a divorce. I couldn't stand another day with her and her kids. Stephanie was simply at the wrong place at the wrong time. I didn't want Stephanie on that trip, but Beverly insisted on all of us going, and it was a holiday! I couldn't leave her!"

Seth got out of the plane, closed the copilot's door, and walked around to the pilot's door.

"Seth, let me go! Now!" Brad pleaded.

Shaking his head, Seth said evenly, "No, you aren't going anywhere. You are going to die the same way Rachel, Elizabeth, and Stephanie died, the same way you killed the boys, the same way you killed Beverly and her boys. And you are going to die in your new private jet. This time you aren't walking away."

Seth opened the rear passenger door and poured the remaining gas onto the seats and the floor of the plane. Before closing the door, he leaned over the back of the pilot's seat and whispered to Brad, "I truly hope you live long enough to feel the pain of every part of your body burning. I disabled the fire alarm before I came into the hangar. Just like no one rescued Rachel and the children, no one will be coming to rescue you, Brad."

He tossed a lit book of matches onto the passenger seat of the plane, closed the door, and walked away without looking back. Before he got to the hangar door, he could hear Brad screaming. He stopped for a brief moment, fighting the temptation to turn around and watch. Then he walked out and closed the door behind him while Brad was still screaming.

Twenty-Eight

County dispatch radioed Sheriff McNeil late Sunday afternoon about a possible fire near Krannert Airport. EMS and the fire department had already been notified and were en route. According to the dispatcher, the person reporting didn't see the fire but saw smoke billowing from the area. While Mac was talking to the dispatcher, he could hear several other calls coming in that the airport was indeed on fire. Mac interrupted the dispatcher and instructed her to immediately notify the county coroner in case there were any bodies that would need to be recovered. He also gave orders to notify the owner-operators of Krannert Airport, Dr. Brad Rivers and Eric Wilkerson, that their business was on fire.

Mac was pulling into his driveway as he finished talking with the dispatcher. The one thing he hated more than getting a call for a domestic was getting called out to investigate a fire. He wasn't looking forward to going back to work, let alone driving to the airport. If he was going to have to go inside the building after the fire department extinguished the blaze, he wanted his waders. Sitting in his driveway, he remembered the waders were at the police department hanging from his coatrack. Slapping the steering wheel in frustration, he backed the car out of the drive and headed back to the station.

The main hangar was still smoldering when he pulled onto the airstrip. The hangar had burned almost to the ground, but at least the fire was out. Getting out of the police cruiser, he scanned the growing crowd, apparently looking for Brad or Eric. Not seeing either of them, he made his way to the entrance of the hangar where the coroner was standing. "Ryan, you actually made it to a scene before me," Mac said to his friend.

Ryan nodded and pointed to the hangar. "I can see a few planes in there. One looks like there could be something in it, but honestly, it could just be the way the plane burned. Maybe the pilot's seat fell forward during the fire. It's still too hot to go inside, and until the building inspector says it's safe, I am happy to speculate out here!"

"That's fine," Mac said as he scanned the ruins. "I can see the planes, but I don't see what you see. It just looks like a burnt plane to me. When it's safe to go in, wait for me and I'll go in with you. Never know if this mess is going to be a crime scene."

Mac walked over to where his deputies were hanging out. "Guys!" he shouted, waving his arms to get their attention. "I don't see any cameras out. You think you can take some pictures while you are standing there?" Mac gestured toward the hangar as he approached. He looked back at the ruins; from where he stood one aircraft did look like something was inside. "Insurance is going to want pictures, and the feds are going to be all over this mess." Mac scanned the crowd again and yelled back at his deputies, "Hey, anyone know if the owners were contacted?" Getting no answer, he threw his hands up in frustration and started pacing in front of the hangar. He turned around toward the entrance of the airport just in time to see a black

BMW racing toward the hangar. He knew the car was either Brad's or Eric's, as both drove the same car.

The BMW screeched to a stop behind one of the police cars; Eric Wilkerson jumped out of the car and ran up to Mac. "What happened? My God, was anyone hurt? I keep trying to call Brad, but I can't reach him!" Eric frantically ran back and forth in front of the building, trying to look inside.

Mac stopped him by reaching out and grabbing his arm. "OK, look, Eric, we can reach him later. Right now, I need you to focus. Was there anyone scheduled to be here today, or anyone that you know could be inside? Anyone who is usually here on a Sunday afternoon?" Mac shook Eric by both shoulders. "Eric, look at me! You need to focus, OK? Is there a schedule? Is there anyone other than Brad you can call to check on the pilots who rented space from you?"

Eric slowly responded, "Uh, let me think, yeah, that's a good idea. I think I have everyone's numbers. I can make some calls. But no, I don't think anyone was scheduled to be here, and we don't keep a calendar or a schedule for the pilots and mechanics. I would have no way of knowing. I mean, the pilots don't schedule their time. If they want to do maintenance, they just use their key and do their thing. They would only schedule a flight plan if they were planning to go anywhere. Otherwise, we don't keep track of anyone. I don't see any cars in the lot, either."

The fire inspector and building inspector approached Mac as Eric was looking up the numbers of the other pilots and staff. "Sheriff, you can go inside. The structure is secure, and the power has been turned off to the hangar. All the wires you see down are dead. Just don't trip over them."

"Inspector, the cause of the fire? Do you think this was an accident or arson?" Mac asked.

"This fire is definitely arson. There is a distinctive burn pattern around one of the planes, and a hot spot. If there hadn't been an accelerant, the fire couldn't have advanced as far as it did. There is evidence the fire started at that plane. Unfortunately, it looks like there is at least one victim," explained the fire investigator. He spoke with a flat, absent tone, as though he were reciting a piece of old news.

Eric stood frozen in his tracks. "Arson?" he stammered. "How—arson—are you sure?"

Twenty-Nine

While Mac and Ryan put on their gear and prepared to go inside, the fire department set up lights to illuminate the inside of the hangar. Yellow police tape was placed around the entire building. Eric was instructed to remain outside until the police and coroner completed their inspections. The hangar was dripping water, and with the lights reflecting off the rafters, it looked eerily like the inside of a gutted steel monster.

Ryan let Mac lead the way into the skeletal remains of the once-elite hangar. They were only a few dozen feet inside when they heard Eric yelling that he had found Brad's car in the back lot of the airstrip. Both men stopped and looked at each other and then at the wreckage of the planes in the hangar. Ryan pointed to the one he had earlier suspected had something in the pilot's seat. Mac nodded his head, and both men headed toward the aircraft. As they got closer, it became obvious to Ryan that someone who had once been very alive and human was now dead in the seat.

"Mac, do you know who owns this plane?" Ryan absently asked as he peered inside the pilot's seat. "Whoever this guy was, he's a crispy critter now. I am going to need the entire front part of this thing moved to the morgue. He isn't going to be easy to get out of this thing, either."

Mac tried to hide the growing unease he felt in the pit of his stomach as he slowly walked over to where the coroner was standing. He peered into the cockpit, shaking his head, and agreed with the coroner. "Uh, yeah, this one can't get any deader, Doc. I have no idea who owns these planes. This could be the owner, someone who rented the plane, or even a mechanic. We need to get Eric in here to tell us which planes are stored where in this mess. I have a bad feeling we are going to find out this is Dr. Rivers. Doc, we need to keep this quiet for as long as possible."

Ryan backed away from the plane and looked around at the rest of debris. "I agree, this has to be kept under wraps. If this is Dr. Rivers, this town will be flooded with the feds, media, and countless lawyers."

"Yep, and until we know, we don't need the company. It's getting late," Ryan said.

"I'll have a few of the deputies set up guard over this place," Mac replied, looking around the rest of the hangar and noticing what the fire inspector had mentioned. "Ryan, look at the burn pattern. The fire inspector said that one of the planes was where the fire started. He didn't say which one. I think this was the start of the fire. Maybe I need to stay here overnight."

"Yeah, I noticed that too." Ryan walked around the back of the plane and then to the passenger side. As he came around to the front of the craft, he turned and looked at the rest of the planes. "Mac, I think you could be right, and the fire started with this plane. This place is mostly concrete and steel. I don't see a lot of damage other than this plane. The sides of the building are gone, the roof is a mess, but the worst of the damage seems to be right here. Which means the fire likely started here, and the roof above this plane is completely gone. What I don't get is how or why the fire was started. Hopefully, this guy can shed some light on what happened tonight."

Thirty

Seth was exhausted when he finally pulled into his driveway. His neighborhood was still dark except for the street lights. He sat in his car for a few minutes, thinking of his conversation with Brad. He already knew most of what Brad had told him, but now he knew that not only had Rachel's husband betrayed her, the church she had loved and the monsignor she thought the world of had also betrayed her. The realization caused him to feel an almost uncontrollable anger. For the sake of his plans, to complete his mission, he needed to maintain control. He *would* maintain control.

He finally got out of the car, his legs stiff and his body sore. With the smell of smoke on his clothes, he slowly and gingerly walked to the front door, fumbling for his keys as he walked. Opening the door, he went inside and paused in the foyer to look at the picture he kept on the entry table. Killing Brad had given him some satisfaction, but it didn't last, and it wasn't enough. There was more work to do, and he needed to be careful not to get linked to either of the bodies. This kill was a first, as he had never killed anyone he could be connected to or who had known him. He had never taken a souvenir, but this time he did. He had taken Brad's cell phone. He didn't need a souvenir, and he hadn't taken it for that purpose. He needed the phone to complete his plans. The monsignor would be calling, and it was one call he didn't want to miss.

He was physically and emotionally exhausted. Before turning to go upstairs, he gently touched the photo. Once in the bathroom he removed his clothes. He stood naked in front of the mirror, staring at himself, not thinking. Everything around him smelled like death—his clothes, his hair, even his skin. He showered and went to bed, but sleep was evasive. All he could think about was Rachel.

They had been childhood friends, and over the years they'd become lovers. When she told him she was pregnant, he had been elated. They both had accepted long ago that their relationship would have to remain as it was. They wanted their child to be raised in a normal home, or as normal as was possible. Rachel had already married Brad, and he was the father of her two older sons. She knew Seth's secret, but she loved him anyway. And how could she not? His last kill was for her. After that night, he had promised her he wouldn't kill again. He kept that promise until Stephanie died.

Lying on the bed under the covers, he allowed himself to cry, not just for Rachel and the boys but for the twins Elizabeth and Stephanie. Killing Brad didn't stop the pain he was feeling as he remembered the night long ago when he'd made his promise to Rachel.

...

"Seth, he isn't breathing! There's blood; he's bleeding!" Rachel yelled. She pushed him away as she struggled to stand. "What did you do? Oh, my God, oh my God. He isn't moving!"

She was crying and yelling at the same time. Her clothes were soiled, her beautiful golden-brown hair matted with mud and leaves. Her tears left streaks down her dirty face. Finally she got to her feet and looked over at Seth. He was calm, standing over her date with a crowbar. He poked at the young man, and when he was satisfied he was dead, he turned to look at Rachel. "I saw you leave with him after the game. I followed you."

Rachel struggled to understand what had just happened. Not just that her date had attacked her, but that Seth had calmly struck him in the head with a crowbar. He didn't seem the least bit upset.

"I don't understand, Seth! I think you killed him," she said softly. She was still slightly unsteady and instinctively reached for him to help her, but then pulled away in fear when he reached for her.

Seth dropped the crowbar and pleaded with her. "Rachel, I'm not going to hurt you. I could never hurt you. You don't understand. He was planning to attack you. This was part of your initiation into the sorority you pledged, and it was part of the fraternity he belonged to! I knew about this; it was all over campus. That's why I followed you! To keep you safe! Look! I can prove it! All the pledges were assigned a number that must be worn on their jackets. Your number is six. It's on your jacket! His fraternity passed out cards with numbers. His number was six! Look in his pockets!"

"No! I don't believe you," Rachel cried, staring in disbelief at Seth.

Seth turned the body over and started going through his pockets, finally finding the card in his front pants pocket. He pulled it out and handed it to Rachel. "I would never hurt you! I could never hurt you! Whatever you think of this guy, he was playing out his frat's game. I am sorry. I really am, but you don't deserve to be treated like this. I just couldn't leave you alone with him, knowing what I knew. I couldn't let him hurt you," he said softly as he lowered his head to avoid her glare.

Rachel took the card from him and carefully examined it. It

was identical to the card she had been given by her sorority as a pledge. She dropped the card and grabbed Seth, hugging him close and crying.

Seth pulled away and took Rachel's face in his hands. "I have to take care of the body," he said.

It was then that Seth told Rachel his secret. He was afraid she would run, tell someone—or worse, hate him. But she didn't. She offered to help him, but he wouldn't let her. He assured her he knew what he was doing and that neither of them would be connected to the body. It was hours later, after the body had been disposed of and Rachel had cleaned herself up, that she convinced Seth to stop killing. Her acceptance surprised him. Instead of his secret driving them apart, it drew them closer. He never completely told her whom or how he killed, or even when he had started killing, and she was content not knowing.

Thirty-One

The following morning the fire and building inspectors cleared the hangar, and the aircraft was disassembled. The body, still sitting in the pilot's seat, was taken to the medical examiner for the autopsy. The rest of the plane was taken to the police crime lab.

Ryan, eating a large, puffy glazed donut and carrying his coffee mug, arrived at the morgue shortly after the body was dropped off. He didn't seem to notice the bits of icing on his cheek. Dead bodies never affected his appetite. However, the stench in the room was enough to make him gag, and the donut he was eating began to taste like a rotting, burnt corpse. He rushed to the trash can and spit out what was left in his mouth and tossed the rest of the donut and his coffee into the can.

The autopsy room smelled like a mixture of wet, burnt leaves and a rotting roadkill in the heat of August. The pilot's seat, with the body still taped to it, had been placed on a low table, which was sitting on top of a large plastic evidence cloth. He would need to remove the body and place it on the slab to perform the autopsy. Walking around the plastic cloth, he examined the remnants of what he was certain was duct tape that had secured the upper arms and torso of the body to the seat. Whoever did this really wanted this guy to not only die but suffer in the process. Staring at the corpse, he realized his job had just gone sideways. He was going to need help getting the body out of the seat. Speaking softly to the corpse, he said, "You remind me of the guy in the wet suit. You must have really pissed off someone. How did you end up here?"

He wasn't sure if Mark was in class or not, but he needed him. If all he could do was leave a voice mail, then that would have to be enough for now. And of course, the call went immediately to voice mail. "This is Dr. Davis," he said. "Mark, what time can you get here? I need your help ASAP! Call me as soon as you get this message." He hung up the phone and muttered, "Figures. That's what I get for hiring medical students."

Before he could put his cell phone back into his pocket, Mark returned his call. The medical school was buzzing with rumors about a body found in the fire at the airport, and Mark wasn't about to pass up the opportunity to work on this case. He was already in the school parking lot, running toward his car, when he called the coroner back. "Got your message, Doc. I am on my way." He disconnected the call before Ryan could reply.

It was all he could do to drive within the speed limit and not run any red lights. Barely slowing down, he whipped into the medical examiner's parking lot and parked his Mustang in the spot next to Ryan's car. He jumped out and ran to the rear door of the morgue and, using his key card to get inside, ran in yelling for Ryan. "Doc! I'm here. Hey, I heard about this guy in class. Whoa, dude, it smells in here!" The odor stopped Mark in his tracks. He slapped his hand over his nose and looked around the room for Ryan.

Ryan came out of his office wearing a mask. Laughing at the med student, he handed him a box of masks. "You should have seen your face, kid! It was priceless! Here, put this on. It won't stop you from smelling it, but at least it will make it a little better. If it smells like peppermint, it's because I sprayed peppermint oil on it. It helps dull the smell. Won't get rid of it, but hey, dull is better than nothing, right? Although you may never eat another candy cane without thinking of this guy."

Ryan and Mark were able to get the body out of the seat after a couple of painstaking hours carefully removing the tape from around the victim and the pilot's seat. The body didn't come off the seat easily. It was as if it had melted into the leather. Ryan had to carefully peal the body away from the leather, leaving bits and pieces of fabric and skin from the corpse. Several samples were taken from the tape, fabric, and skin as well as the seat. What was left of the body, still in a sitting position, was placed in a CT scanner. After films were taken, it was placed on top of the autopsy slab. "Mark, look, you may want to leave for this part. I need the body to be flat to do the autopsy."

Mark nodded his head. "OK, yes, but I am not leaving. So when will the rigor settle?"

"It won't. I need to break the limbs, and even for me this is rough. I will understand if you want to take a break, no pun intended."

"OK, I get it. Hmm, yeah, I'll stay. I mean, someday this could be me doing one like this, and the guy is already dead. It is a guy?" Mark softly asked.

"Yes, it's a guy, Mark."

Ryan explained the process to break the limbs at the joint, while at the same time preserving the long bones. Once the two men had the body flat, additional x-rays were taken, including a panoramic film of the jaw.

"I think I know who this guy is, and I am hoping and praying I'm wrong. The quickest way to find out is a dental match. This guy has veneers on his front teeth. We can get this to the local dentists today or tomorrow at the latest. I'm ready to start the formal autopsy. Do you need a break? I know I do," he said thoughtfully.

"Um, yeah, sure, I could use a soda." Mark paused, looking at the body sitting eerily on the slab. "Doc, who do you think this guy is? Damn, what a way to go, huh?"

The men went to the employee break room where Ryan kept a supply of Diet Coke in the fridge. Everyone who worked there knew he didn't care who drank the soda, as long as the last one wasn't taken. He peered inside the soda box and was relieved to see the box was half full. He took out two and tossed one to Mark. They sat in silence drinking their sodas.

"Are you ready, kid?" Ryan quietly asked, breaking the silence. This body was getting to him. He couldn't put his finger on it yet, but something about this guy was just wrong. It wasn't that he died in a fire, and it wasn't that he was strapped to the pilot's seat. For all he knew, this was a mob hit. There was simply something else, and Ryan couldn't shake the feeling that whatever it was, it was close.

Mark nodded his head and tossed the empty soda can into the trash. "Let's do it, Doc!"

Ryan led the way to autopsy room, stopping first to put on a pair of blue paper overalls, blue foot covers, and a blue paper hat. Mark did the same. Once they were each dressed, with masks in place, Ryan motioned for Mark to turn on the recorder. Ryan stated the date and time for the recorder and gave a brief description of the body.

The limbs hadn't been as difficult to break as Ryan had expected. Both he and Mark carefully removed whatever clothing they could. The body was fairly well burnt, and it wasn't possible to remove all the clothing. Before Ryan performed the standard Y incision, he took photos of the corpse, but stopped when he noticed something unusual.

"Mark, come over here and tell me what you think of this guy's upper legs and chest. Do you notice anything out of the ordinary?"

"Doc, this whole guy is out of the ordinary!" Mark said. Although visibly shaken, Mark was trying to sound confident. "I don't know what I am looking for. It just looks burnt!"

Ryan pointed to the corpse. "Take a closer look at the legs and chest. I'll have to send samples of these areas to the state crime lab, but if I am right—and I have no reason to doubt my findings—there are places on his legs and chest that look like the fire started in each area, then were extinguished and started a second time."

Ryan leaned closer to the right upper leg, using a magnifying lens to assist him in his evaluation. "It's barely noticeable, but one of the burns has a layered appearance. The only way this happens is if he was set on fire and then, for whatever sick reason, the fire was extinguished and restarted in the exact same place!" Ryan exclaimed while removing cloth and tissue samples from the legs and chest and placing them in a steel tray for Mark to label for evidence.

"You think he was set on fire? Couldn't the same thing happen if the fire started and he caught fire in different areas at different times?" Mark asked as he labeled the samples.

"No, this could only happen if different parts of his body were set on fire at different times. I think he was the start of the fire. Think about it: Why was this guy duct taped to the seat? There appear to be areas that burned, but not as much as other areas. For example, this area on his right upper thigh. The clothes appear to have burned in a small circle, but the tissue under it isn't. Yet the rest of his leg is burned. How did his pants burn, yet the skin under the pants didn't burn, but the rest of the upper leg did? It looks like somehow this part was on fire, then the fire went out, and the rest of this started from another area. If I am right, this guy was tortured before he finally died. We need to find out who he is, or was, and soon."

Ryan finished the autopsy and gave his initial cause of death as fire. He turned off the recorder and said to Mark, "Let's get him into a body bag. The dental films will go out tomorrow. Until then, we wait. And I need to make a phone call."

It was already late in the day when Ryan tried to reach Mac. If he didn't answer his cell, he would try the sheriff's office. Just as he expected, Mac didn't answer, and he wasn't at the office. After leaving messages for Mac to call him, he locked up and went home.

...

Mac was intentionally ignoring the calls from Ryan. He had spent the entire night of the fire with his deputies at the airport, and that was after spending the day at work. He waited until the body had been sent to the morgue and the crime lab had finished processing the hangar before going back to his office. As soon as he could leave the next day, he went home. After more than twenty-four hours at work, he needed a break. When he got home he showered and went straight to bed. As exhausted as he was, he was surprised that he had difficulty sleeping. Finally he did fall asleep, and when he did, he dreamt of the fire.

Thirty-Two

The obnoxious iPhone alarm woke Mac up from a restless sleep. He was still very tired but also grateful to be awake. The nightmare still lingering in his consciousness, he slowly pulled himself out of bed, tossing the blankets to the floor, and stumbled into the bathroom. There were times when he looked into the mirror that he barely recognized himself. This was one of those mornings. He looked haggard and old. "Time to retire and move to a warm beach somewhere," he muttered to himself.

Mac showered quickly and headed back into town. Instead of going to the sheriff's office, he stopped for donuts and coffee and then went directly to the medical examiner's office. Ryan would be there early, and he knew Ryan would be irritated with him for ignoring his calls. He also knew the quickest way to his friend's forgiveness was a donut and a cup of hot coffee from his favorite mom-and-pop café.

Ryan pulled into the parking lot just after Mac had parked the police cruiser. He watched as Mac held the bag of donuts from the car window for him to see. "Look, you asshole, it's going to take more than a donut for you to get off my shit list," Ryan laughingly yelled at him as he walked over to the police cruiser.

Mac got out of the cruiser and held up his offering of coffee. "So, will hot coffee from Sara's get me off that shit list?" Mac joked as he handed Ryan the coffee.

"Yeah, yeah, it's a start," he replied as he waved his hand. "Nice of you to finally show up! Been trying to call you since yesterday. We need to talk! But first I want a donut, and I need that coffee. Yesterday and last night were bad. Couldn't sleep. Kept thinking about this guy and how he died. Hell of a way to go. Come on, let's go inside. I'll give you all the details."

Once inside, Ryan led the way to his office. "Thank God I had a medical student to help with this one," he said. After making sure they were alone, he closed the door and explained his theory to Mac.

"You think this guy was set on fire, then the fire was put out, and then he was set on fire again? That doesn't make any sense." Mac was struggling to wrap his head around his friend's theory. "That means this guy was tortured and intentionally killed. Plus, you think—and correct me if I'm misunderstanding you—you think this murder is related to the detective's murder? How? He wasn't stuffed in a wet suit—or in anything, for that matter. His cause of death wasn't hidden, and nothing postmortem happened to him. I don't see how it's related."

"Right. He wasn't stuffed into a wet suit; he was duct-taped to a seat and set on fire. So the body was contained just prior to death, instead of after death. And yes, nothing happened to the body after he died, but I still think somehow these two are connected. It's just a feeling, Mac. I have been doing this for a long time. Somehow these two are related. Piecing this all together is up to you and your guys." Ryan waited for Mac to say something.

"Yeah, it is up to us to put this together. And it does sound like a complicated mess. OK, let's go with your theory. If these two are related, then we have a serial killer in or around our little town," Mac said, downing the last of his coffee and tossing the cup in the trash. "We need to find this guy's identity."

"Yes, about that. I think I know who he is, Mac. And I hope to God I'm wrong. I sent his dental films to the local dentists in town and to a couple in Boston. I should have the results in a couple of days at the most," Ryan replied.

"Want to clue me in? Who do you think he is?" asked Mac.

"Brad Rivers. I think he's Dr. Brad Rivers. As of the fire, his business partner, Eric Wilkerson, who is also his lawyer, couldn't reach him. He said all the calls were going to voice mail." Ryan sighed and took another drink from his coffee before continuing. "Think about it. Who else could this guy be?"

Mac slowly nodded his head in understanding. "This is the same Dr. Rivers who recently crashed a plane in Florida that killed his wife and daughter?"

"That's right. And that wasn't the first accident. He crashed a plane a few years ago that killed his first wife and all their children but one. A daughter named . . . I think her name was Stephanie. This latest crash was his second wife and the surviving child from the first accident. Maybe someone had it in for him?" Ryan asked. "I mean, what are the odds of crashing two planes and surviving?"

"Ryan, I can see where you think the bodies are similar, but I don't see a connection between the pilot doctor and the detective. Remember, we haven't had a positive ID of the body yet. I don't want to assume anything," Mac said with a mouthful of donut.

Ryan smiled. "Mac, my man, you need more coffee! I can draw the line for you if you need me to," he laughed as he jokingly slapped Mac's shoulder. "Eric Wilkerson is the connection, or his former girlfriend is the connection. Bear with me for a moment. The new attorney in town is Emily Bridges. She was once engaged to Eric Wilkerson, who just happens to be business partners with Dr. Rivers.

She also once worked with Detective Connard, the body she found in the surf. Now, Mac, I am the coroner, not a cop, and I don't believe in coincidences. I'm damn sure you don't either!"

Mac nodded his head and agreed with him. "OK, that is a strange connection. Before we pursue this angle, let's make sure your dead body is Dr. Rivers. If it is Dr. Rivers, who would want him dead? I mean, think about it: He ran a successful plastic surgery center, his business at the airport seems busy, and his partner is a lawyer. Not to mention that he never had so much as a speeding ticket. So if your theory is correct, then someone wanted him dead, and someone wanted him to suffer. Did anything else show up on the autopsy?"

Ryan leaned back in his chair. "Even though he suffered severe burns, I was able to get some organ and tissue samples. So far, nothing. The toxicology results were sent to the state, but the preliminary results were negative. Hey, did you have a chance to go over the crime scene photos?"

Mac set his coffee cup on the desk. "No, I spent the first night at the airport with my men. I think I slept most of yesterday! And this morning, I literally came directly here after going to Sara's for donuts and coffee. Are the photos uploaded?"

"Yeah, they are ready. From what I can tell, the fire started with the plane. We still need to get the fire inspector's report. But it's pretty obvious the fire started with the guy who was duct taped to the pilot's seat."

Ryan turned his computer for Mac to see and opened the file containing the pictures. Nothing looked out of the ordinary until he opened the file containing Dr. Rivers's car. Ryan pointed to the screen and excitedly asked, "Mac, do you see that? What the hell?" Stuffed in the driver's window frame was a small plastic bag. Ryan zoomed in on the baggie until they both saw what appeared to be an old, yellowed newspaper clipping of a birth announcement.

Mac leaned in to get a closer look. "I can't make out anything other than that's a birth announcement. Hmmm, Ryan, I don't want to jump to conclusions, but I'm beginning to think maybe you're on to something. And don't let this go to your head!"

"Now, that will be a first, buddy! Can't imagine being right," Ryan chuckled as he shook his head at Mac. "Given how many times in my career I have never been wrong! All kidding aside, finding the identity of this man is my first priority."

"I agree. I need to know ASAP if that body is Dr. Rivers, and honestly, I have a very bad feeling it is. I also need to know today what is on the newspaper announcement. I'll be in touch."

Mac hurriedly got out of his chair and left the medical examiner's office. He pulled out of the parking lot so fast his tires squealed. He needed to have a chat with Eric Wilkerson and Emily Bridges, and the sooner the better. He couldn't afford to wait for the completion of the autopsy report.

Thirty-Three

"Dr. Rivers, finally you answer the phone," Tedesco said flatly. He didn't like to wait, and he most assuredly did not like to have his calls ignored. Regardless of the man's family's funerals, Brad was more than aware of his obligations to Tedesco, and ignoring Tedesco wasn't in his best interest.

"Hmmm, yes, my apologies, Monsignor," Seth replied carefully. He wondered if Tedesco would notice the difference between his voice and Brad's. Surprisingly, he didn't seem to.

"I have left several messages for you. As you know, we are running short on time. This next charter needs to happen within the next few days, or a week at the very most. It may very well be our last." Tedesco leaned back in his chair. He was annoyed that his calls hadn't been returned quickly, and this delay in response time was unusual. Brad usually returned his calls within minutes of missing a call. "I will not tolerate any further delays, Dr. Rivers. You are aware of your obligation as well as our expectations."

"I don't need to be reminded. However, I won't be able to fly this time. Eric Wilkerson will be the pilot, but I assure you, I will be there to ensure the charter is a success," Seth quickly replied. But this time he felt the monsignor did notice a difference with his voice.

Tedesco paused. Something was off with Brad. "Dr. Rivers, please accept my condolences on the loss of your wife and daughter. I certainly hope you aren't getting sick. You sound different today." The monsignor leaned forward in his chair, his elbows on his desk, intently listening to the voice at the other end of the call.

"Yes, of course, everything is all right. My throat is still sore from a breathing tube. I was on a vent for just a short time, and it seems to have left my voice sounding harsh. Perhaps that is what you notice." Seth wasn't sure the monsignor was going to believe him.

"Dr. Rivers, do you recall the first time we met?" Tedesco paused, listening for any indication he was not talking to Brad Rivers. "Perhaps you can alleviate my concerns and tell me about that first day in St. Peter's Basilica?"

"Of course, yes, Monsignor. However, I believe you are mistaken. We did go to St. Peter's Basilica, but it was on the second day. The first day my wife Rachel and I met you was at the entrance to the Pantheon," he replied quickly. Years ago, Rachel had not only told him all about her beloved trip to Rome and meeting the monsignor, she had shown him pictures of her trip. For Rachel, meeting a Vatican monsignor was the highlight of the trip. "I hope I have alleviated your concerns," he said as he cautiously awaited the monsignor's response.

"Very good answer, Dr. Rivers. May I strongly suggest that from this time forward, when I call, you answer your phone? I will be moving forward on this end, and to be candid, Doctor, I don't appreciate delays. You wouldn't want to disappoint me. Don't mistake me as having a forgiving nature because I am a priest." With that he disconnected the call.

Before he could place a call to his associate Liam, there was knock on his office door. Without waiting for a response, the secretary to the pope opened the door and walked into his office. Bowing slightly, he said, "Monsignor Tedesco, the council has requested an update regarding the final steps you are taking to ensure repatriations to the victims."

Monsignor Tedesco nodded his head understandingly. "Of course. What time is the council meeting?"

"Two p.m., Thursday, the fourth of November. I was instructed to return with an acceptance if you are ready or a request for an extension." The secretary waited for a response.

Standing up from his chair, Tedesco replied, "Please inform the council that my report will be ready on the fourth of November at two o'clock."

The secretary bowed slightly and walked out of the office.

Tedesco waited until he was certain he was alone and then locked his office door before making a quick call to Liam. He had one week to get the gold out of the old church. "Liam, Tedesco here. We need to step up the retrieval from Nykøbing Mors. Can you meet me there tomorrow morning? I made arrangements to fly out immediately. I will be at the train station by eight a.m." Tedesco wasn't asking. He was giving Liam instructions, and he expected nothing less than an agreement.

Liam had met Tedesco when he was in seminary. Unfortunately for Liam, he had been asked to leave after he was discovered smuggling hashish from Turkey to the Vatican City with the intent of selling it to his seminary classmates. He wasn't a user, but he was very good at seeing an opportunity and taking advantage of it. He may have been removed from seminary, but his career in smuggling had just begun, and so with it his partnership with Tedesco.

"I was waiting for your call," Liam said. "The media is very excited about the upcoming repatriations. Rumor has it the Nazi gold has been found, or at the least, some of the gold. Monsignor, is this true?" Even though they were partners, and had been for decades, Liam was still very respectful of Tedesco's position and always referred to him by his title.

Tedesco didn't answer his question. "I will meet you at the seven ten R train at Nakskov Street, Nykøbing Mors. It leaves every hour on the eighteenth minute. Be on the ten eighteen. I will go over the details once we are on the train." He didn't wait for Liam to respond. If there were any complications, he knew Liam would contact him.

Thirty-Four

Tedesco's flight landed on time, and as expected, his car and driver were waiting for him. The driver was an older man with the type of leathered skin you would expect from a fisherman, not a chauffeur. His snow-white hair stuck out from below a well-worn leather cap that he tipped in respect toward his charge. "Good morning, Monsignor. Where to for this trip?" he asked.

"Just the train station, and good morning to you as well. You are looking well as usual," Tedesco replied.

"Thank you, Monsignor. We shall be there in under fifteen minutes. Do you wish to schedule a pickup time for your return?"

"I am not certain what time I will return. However, as soon as I know, I will contact you. You can drop me off at the ticket booth," instructed Tedesco as he reached over the seat to hand the driver a tip.

It was midmorning, and the train station wasn't busy. Tedesco purchased the 10:18 ticket and waited patiently for the train to arrive. While he waited, he cautiously scanned the platform, looking for Liam.

"Aw, there you are, Monsignor. I saw you approach. I am surprised you didn't see me first. I am probably the tallest person on the platform. Were you enjoying your wait?" Liam asked. He had approached Tedesco from behind, and for a man with an imposing size, he was graceful enough to blend in with most crowds.

Tedesco laughed at Liam's comments and replied jokingly, "You are getting better at approaching without making noise. I commend you, my friend! We should find a car with few to no people. There is much to discuss."

Tedesco switched from jovial to serious in an instant, and nodded his head toward the train as it pulled into the station. Without speaking further, both men boarded and walked toward the back of the train where they were certain to find a car with few or no people. And as luck would have it, they were able to sit alone in the last train car.

Looking over his shoulder and making certain they were indeed alone, Tedesco finally felt safe enough to talk. "Liam, now to answer your earlier question, yes, I have located a small vault in an old church in Nykøbing Mors. Inside the vault is the long-rumored missing Nazi gold. I have no idea how much gold there is, or if it's even all the gold. All I know is that there is a lot of gold. Enough for us to remove, and enough to give back for the reparations. Here is a sample of what I found. I only removed one bag."

Tedesco reached into the inner pocket of his coat, removed a small cloth bag, and handed it to Liam. "This is only a small sample of what is in the vault. This bag alone contained fifty coins. Look at the markings on each side of the coin. There is no doubt this is Nazi gold. The vault contains much more than these bags of gold coins. There are also several stacks of gold bars and what appear to be hundreds of pieces of art, including paintings, sculptures, and other things wrapped in paper. I didn't have the time to unwrap those items. But for them to be in the vault, they must be valuable."

Liam had been turning the coin over and over in his hand while Tedesco spoke. He waited until he was certain Tedesco was finished. "Where is the vault?" Over the years, he and Tedesco had smuggled several shipments out of Germany, Austria, and Italy. "I heard about the reparations. When is this supposed to take place? If this vault is inside a church, is there a priest we need to concern ourselves with?"

"There is an elderly priest and a nun. However, the nun has every Tuesday off, and today is Tuesday. We only have today to empty the vault. I have given this a lot of thought, and the only way to get into the vault is if the priest is gone. He isn't going to leave, so unfortunately, we have to with deal this. At his age, if he were to pass in his sleep, no one would consider anything other than natural causes. I expect you to manage this. I also expect that however you manage this, the priest does not suffer. No reason for a good man to suffer," Tedesco said softly. Killing the priest was not sitting well with him, but he couldn't think of any other way to remove the items from the vault without being seen. "It has gotten colder in the last few weeks."

Nodding his head in agreement, Liam responded, "Yes, that will make things easier. I assure you the priest will not suffer. Given the lower temperatures, his body will remain intact, and he will be found in his bed."

"We are almost at our stop. Were you able to obtain a truck for our use today?" Tedesco asked.

"Of course. Everything we need for today has been discretely arranged."

The train stopped and both men exited, with Liam leading the way to the truck. True to his word, sitting in the parking lot was a white midsize panel truck. Once inside, Tedesco breathed a sigh of relief. He wasn't a stranger to having someone killed or even killing someone himself, but he always tried not to involve the Church in his outside activities, and that included killing a priest.

"Here is the location of the church," Tedesco said, handing Liam a piece of paper. "If memory serves me correctly, we are only twenty-two kilometers from the church. The priest isn't expecting us."

Instead of using the truck's GPS or his cell phone navigator, Liam removed a map from the glove box. "We go my way, Monsignor." He started the truck and easily made the trip to the church.

"Drop me off at the gate," said Tedesco. "Give me a few minutes to speak with the Father and then you can come inside. Don't forget, this man is not to suffer. We understand each other?" Tedesco asked.

"Of course. I give you my word," Liam assured him.

Tedesco walked to the church, and instead of ringing the bell, he slowly opened the exterior door and stepped into the vestibule. Opening the doors of the narthex, he called out to Father Joseph. He waited inside for the elder priest to respond. Not getting a response, he entered the sanctuary and made his way to the office of the priest. Without knocking, he entered the office. Father Joseph was sitting at his desk and looked up when Tedesco entered.

"Monsignor Tedesco, I have been waiting for you."

"Waiting for me? What do you mean?" Tedesco asked in genuine surprise.

"Monsignor, I am an old man, but I am neither a forgetful man nor a demented man. I have been the only priest for this church in close to fifty years. I know what is in the basement. Did you think I did not know what you had found? Did you think I did not know you did not report those findings to the Vatican?" Father Joseph coughed frequently as he spoke. His voice was hoarse and soft.

"Father, if this is so, why did you not report the contents of the basement yourself?" Tedesco asked as he walked closer to the desk. "Why did you keep it a secret all these years?"

Shaking his head, the old priest replied, "My purpose was to protect the contents of the vault. It was never my place to question the reason for its secrecy. It is also not my place today to report the contents of the vault, nor is it my place to make possible false allegations about a Vatican monsignor. I knew you would either return to remove the items for the reparations or you would remove the items for yourself. 'Cursed is he who seizes his neighbor's inheritance and takes for himself.' You recall your teachings of Deuteronomy chapter nineteen verse fourteen? If you remove these items, you will be cursed, even if you remove a single item."

Father Joseph looked into the eyes of the monsignor, waiting for a glimpse of remorse. Seeing nothing, he said, "I see you have brought someone to assist you." He pointed toward the door to where Liam stood patiently watching the two men. "Are you going to introduce me to the man who intends to kill me, or am I going to find out his name after I die?"

Tedesco placed his hand on the shoulder of the aging priest. "Father, it is with great regret this has to be the end."

Using the desk to support himself, Father Joseph stood up. "Great regret, I doubt, as greed has consumed your soul."

"Ah, a sermon I don't need, Father." Gesturing toward the door, he continued, "This is my associate, Liam. He will assist you to your bed." Tedesco waved Liam into the office. "He will ensure you are comfortable."

Gently taking Father Joseph by the arm, Liam assisted Father Joseph to his room.

"So, Liam, is it? Good to know who is ending my life." The two men walked the remainder of the way in silence. Once in his bedroom, Liam helped Father Joseph change clothes and even carefully hung his robes according to the instructions given to him.

Liam poured a glass of water from the table in the old priest's room. "Father Joseph, take these capsules. They will help you get comfortable."

Taking the capsules with a glass of water, Father Joseph recited 2 Samuel 22:3: "My God is my rock, in whom I take refuge, my shield and the horn of my salvation. He is my stronghold, my refuge and my savior—from violent people you save me." He handed Liam the empty glass, settled comfortably in the bed, and, propped up with pillows, just before closing his eyes, he took one last look around his room and sighed softly.

Liam remained with the priest until he passed. He surprised himself when he felt a little sorrow as he removed all evidence that he had been in the room. Before exiting, he looked back at the dead priest and softy muttered, "May you lie in peace for eternity."

Liam gently closed Father Joseph's door and made his way back to the priest's office. Tedesco was already in the basement when he returned to the office. "Monsignor?" Liam yelled through the open door as he made his way down the steps. Layers of dust filled the air as Tedesco removed the brittle paper and cloth coverings on various paintings and crystal glassware. "Monsignor, we may need to wear face masks. How can you breathe in there?" Liam asked.

Tedesco turned around and pointed to the scarf covering his mouth and nose. "Already ahead of you! Pull your shirt up over your nose until the dust settles. While you were with Father Joseph, the van was delivered. I have loaded a few paintings, but as you can see, we haven't begun to scratch the surface of this vault." Tedesco leaned closer to Liam and softly asked, "How is Father Joseph? I assume all is taken care of."

Liam nodded. "All is well, Monsignor. There were no issues, and there will be no issues."

"Good to hear," Tedesco replied. "Now let's get the vault loaded."

Tedesco and Liam took the better part of the afternoon emptying the vault. Once the vans were loaded, they made their way to the airport where they would meet with their American friends, the pilots Dr. Brad Rivers and Eric Wilkerson.

Thirty-Five

Sheriff McNeil didn't waste any time leaving the morgue. In fact, he left so fast Ryan was left wondering what he had missed. He turned back to the crime scene photos, and this time he took a closer look. While he was scrolling through the pics, he heard the side door to the morgue open and the soft footsteps of his part-time clerk. Before he could call out to her, she announced her arrival to whomever was in the morgue.

"Hey, everybody, I am here. Don't no one get up for me!" Miss Van yelled. His clerk was an older black woman with a loud, booming voice that carried a southern accent. She had a heart of gold and took care of the staff as if they were her children.

Ryan yelled back to her, "Miss Van, was a file from last night's fire delivered?" He waited for a response, and when he didn't get one, he got up and walked to the front. "I have been so busy with the guy,

I haven't had a chance to check."

Miss Van was just getting settled at her desk.

"Is there anything for me on your desk?" Ryan gently asked her again as he approached her desk.

"I haven't even put down my coffee, and you go barking at me," she laughed as she scolded him. "Let me get settled and I'll check. You just wait over there!"

Miss Van put her sweater over the chair, placed her coffee next to the phone, and then sat down at her desk. She reached over to the stack of envelopes and quickly ruffled though them. She easily found a large yellow envelope with "Attention Coroner" stamped across the middle. "I think this is probably what you're looking for, Doc," she said as she handed the envelope to him.

Taking the large manila envelope, he said, "Thank you, Miss Van." He turned and hurriedly made his way back to his office. Before leaving the front of the morgue, he hollered back to her, "Thank you again! You know I appreciate you, and enjoy that coffee!"

Ryan placed the large manila envelope perfectly in the middle of his desk. Next to "Attention Coroner" was a yellow sticky note. Written on the note was the time and date the envelope had been delivered. He had told his staff countless times that using sticky notes was not a proper way to communicate, but whatever, he had the file. He quickly opened it, spilling the contents in a neat pile on his desk. He carefully went through each photo, not looking for anything in particular but looking for something. This fire, this body were bothering him. The way the pilot died bothered him. He didn't need to wait on the identification of the body. This guy was tortured, and it was obvious that whoever did it had intended to kill Dr. Rivers and wanted him to suffer. He had no doubt the body was Dr. Rivers. And that bothered him too. He knew the history of the prior accidents involving Dr. Rivers and his family. It was simply a matter of time before someone took out the doctor.

Then he found what he was looking for at the bottom of the

stack. Taking a magnifying glass from his desk, he carefully looked at the news clipping that had been placed in the car window. It was definitely a birth announcement, but it was for Dr. Rivers's youngest children, the twins Elizabeth and Stephanie.

"Miss Van!" Ryan hollered louder than he had intended. "Hey, do you know anything about Stephanie Rivers? That would be Dr. Rivers's daughter?"

He knew Miss Van hated it when he yelled for her from his office, and she would either call him by phone or ignore him. This time, however, he heard her chair creak as she got up, and he listened as she slowly and carefully made her way down the hall toward his office. He knew she must be mad at him, as it took great effort for her to walk. Her knees were bent from age and weight. He guessed she probably was in dire need of a joint replacement. He also knew if she was walking to his office, he'd better pay close attention.

"Now, Doc, how many times do I have to ask you not to yell at me from this nasty, dark hole in the building that you call your office? You know how bad my knees hurt! You know how hard it is for me to get up and out of that chair and walk down this hall to your office! I ain't some young thing that's gonna run up and down these here halls, either." Pointing at the phone on his desk, she continued to scold him. "You want me, you call me on that phone you carry and the phone I sit next to. I will answer." Shaking her finger at him and smiling, she continued, "And, don't you be yelling at me from this office." Bracing herself against the door jam, she waited for him to reply.

"Yes, Miss Van. I won't do it again," he said looking up from the photos.

"Oh yes you will, and I'll be here to make you shape up! Now, what was so important that I had to get up out of my chair and walk all the way back here?"

"Miss Van, I am sorry. Forgive me?"

Chuckling, she said, "Now you know I do."

"Thank you. Do you know about Stephanie Rivers?"

Steadying herself with the doorknob and walking farther into his office, she accepted the photo from the coroner. Examining the photo, she said, "This is Stephanie Rivers? The little girl who died in the plane crash? I don't know anything more than anyone else! All I know is what I heard on the news. She was Dr. Rivers's youngest, and unfortunately, she died in the last plane crash. Awful life for that child. Can you imagine? She loses her mother, brothers, and twin sister in the first crash and then dies in such a horrific way in yet another crash! That poor child!" Shaking her head in sadness, she said, "She never had no one looking after her." She handed the birth announcement photo back to the coroner. "It's almost as if she was never destined to live. Never had a chance, that one." Sighing, she turned and ambled back down the hall to the dispatch booth.

Leaning back in his chair, Ryan ran his hands through his hair. The events of the previous few days were wearing on him. He knew that soon all of this would fall into place, but something still puzzled him. Something in the photos.

He was on his second cup of coffee when he noticed what was wrong. The police photographer who had turned in the first set of prints had taken a photo of Dr. Rivers's car. There was nothing stuck in the driver's side window, nothing on the windshield. Ryan poured through the rest of the photos until he found the photo with the birth announcement stuck in Dr. Rivers's car window. Comparing the two photos, he slowly realized the old newspaper clipping had to have been put on the car by someone after the fire was extinguished. Sitting back in his chair, he also realized only one person could have placed the clipping in the car window.

Thirty-Six

Ryan heard the door to the morgue open and knew who was entering the space just by listening to the footsteps. He didn't wait for him to speak. He was still somewhat hoping he was wrong. He would know soon enough.

"You killed them all, didn't you?" asked Ryan. It was more of statement than a question. "I just don't understand why," he stammered. "You didn't even know these people."

Ryan was confused but continued stumbling for the words to express how stunned he was to learn that his closest friend for years—who was also the sheriff of his home community—could commit such heinous acts of violence against seemingly innocent people. "Stop staring at me and explain this to me," he said. "Why . . . ? Are you planning to kill me too?"

Slowly shaking his head no, Mac said, "Ryan, you're a good friend and a good man. And for those reasons, I'll answer your questions. To answer your last question first, believe it or not, I have no intention of killing you. Now for the first question, I may not have known all of them on a personal basis, but I did know of them, and all of them are intricately related to each other."

He waited for a response, and seeing nothing more than stunned disbelief on Ryan's face, he continued with his story. "Before I became Mac, and long before I ever moved here, my name was Seth Richards. Dr. Rivers's first wife, Rachel, was my closest friend growing up, and eventually we became lovers, but that was after she married Brad and after she had the boys. She eventually became pregnant with Stephanie and Elizabeth . . . my children . . . my daughters. Whom he killed. He didn't just kill one person, Ryan. He killed Rachel and his sons; he killed his second wife, Beverly, and her kids; and of course . . . Stephanie and Elizabeth. Are you keeping count? I have. He killed eight people, at least eight people, that I know of."

"Why didn't Rachel just get a divorce? You two could have gotten married and raised your children. Hell, she could have gotten a decent settlement and possibly custody of her sons."

"Maybe, but I wasn't calling myself Seth. I changed my name after college. You forget that I was a police officer in Boston long before I accepted this job. Dr. Rivers has—or had—enough money to discover not only who I really am but also Rachel's secrets. That discovery would have cost her the children."

Seth removed his gun from his holster and motioned for Ryan to stand up. "Grab your coat, a blanket, and anything else you may need to stay warm and, most importantly, alive."

Ryan was even more confused. "You really aren't going to kill me? How are you going to ensure I don't talk to anyone or call the state police? Look, buddy, we have been friends for a long time, but you know me, I can't keep quiet about this. There are too many dead bodies, too many questions, and the bottom line is . . . I just can't stay quiet."

Seth was still pointing the gun at him. "I know, but I also know

I am not going to kill a good man, much less a good friend, even if that means risking exposure. Besides, Ryan, you aren't going to be found for at least twelve hours, and that's all the time I need to finish. After I am done, I don't really care what happens to me." He tossed Ryan's coat to him. "Put the coat on, and get a couple of blankets off the gurneys. I don't want you to freeze to death or lose a finger." He smiled lightly.

Ryan backed up to the gurney and grabbed the blankets that were lying on top. "OK, uh, Mac . . . or Seth, is it? I understand why you killed the doctor, but I don't understand the rest. Why the police detective? And how did you get the body to the beach without anyone seeing you? Oh, and how on earth did you know the lawyer would find him?"

"To be honest, the lawyer finding him was purely a coincidence. A perfect coincidence. I couldn't have planned it better, but it was, nonetheless, a coincidence. As for the rest, you forget who I am and where I used to work. I am the sheriff. Who do you think closed the beach that day? I closed the beach. Detective Connard was a colleague of mine back in the day. I think we went to the academy together. Not that it matters," Seth absently added. "I invited him to interview for a job. Of course, the job didn't exist. Before you ask, there is no record of my invitation. I arranged an accidental run-in with him in Boston a few weeks before he came out here for the interview. Our conversation was completely verbal, and I insisted he tell no one under the guise that the job wasn't posted, it was his if he wanted it, and all he had to do was keep his mouth shut. Which he did. He was easy to kill. And by the way, good job on discovering 'death by burking.' I wasn't expecting you to figure that out so fast. After he was dead, I lubed him up in motor oil and stuffed him in the wet suit. I had the body in my truck when I closed the beach. It was just a matter of dumping him."

"But why him? How does he fit?" Ryan kept asking questions in the hopes that one of his residents would walk into the morgue.

"You're stalling, Ryan, but I expected no less. He fits because he was connected to Rachel. In an indirect way, but he still fits. He worked for the lawyer, Emily. He wasn't a good cop, and he certainly wasn't a good person. He knowingly turned in a false confession that eventually led to the death of an innocent kid.

"Your next question I will ask for you. How did Emily fit in, you wonder? She hired him and then lied about hiring him, and as latent justice would have it, she was sued by the family of the kid. She lost her job and almost lost her license to practice law. But most importantly, and this is what matters to me the most, it's not the kid. I am not a vigilante. Emily was Rachel's best friend, and when Rachel came to her for guidance and told her in confidence that she suspected Brad and Eric of smuggling, Emily not only ignored her, she violated her trust. She told Eric, and Eric told Brad. Brad's first plane crash was the following week. Even after Rachel died, Emily refused to bring charges against the doctor, and she refused to investigate the case. Stephanie would be alive today if Emily hadn't betrayed Rachel's trust. Possibly Rachel would be alive too."

Seth finished his story and let out a sigh of relief. "I am just curious, Ryan, what gave me away? I am always careful."

"'Always'? What does that mean, 'always'? Are there more than these killings?" Ryan hesitantly asked.

"Of course there is, my friend." Seth softly laughed. "I don't think you want to know all the skeletons in my closet, and I am not prepared to divulge everything, at least not tonight. Now, I asked you a question, and given that I have answered yours, you need to answer mine. How did you figure this out?"

"The picture. The one by your front door," Ryan answered, shaking his head. "I have seen that picture many times, and something about it always bothered me. You know, Mac, uh, I mean Seth. It is Seth, isn't it?"

Seth nodded his head. "Yes, it is."

"OK, Seth. At first I thought it was a picture of you and your sister. 'Perhaps she's dead, and that's why he never talks about her.' That's what I told myself. The state searched Dr. Rivers's home, you remember. You were there. A box of papers, flight records, and even some old photos were removed. One old photo was of a young girl and boy standing in front of a house. I knew I had seen that picture before, and it finally came to me. I had seen that photo before because it was one of you with the same young girl. The photo was in your house, on your table, in your foyer. It wasn't a photo of your sister; it was a shrine to Rachel."

"Hmmm, I didn't think you had noticed the photo. It doesn't matter. Get the coat on. As much as I would enjoy talking to you more, my friend, I have to leave." Seth opened the morgue cooler and motioned for Ryan to go inside.

Ryan put the coat on, picked up the blankets, and walked toward the open door. "You are really going through with this, aren't you? I suppose this will be the last time I see you."

Seth reached into his jacket, pulled out a handful of pocket hand warmers, and tossed them to Ryan. "Use these sparingly. I know you probably don't believe me, but I would hate to find out something happened to you. If you look closely in those blankets, you will find a small flashlight. I will send someone to open the door once I am finished."

Looking at his old friend standing in front of the cooler door, Seth felt a flash of sadness. They had been friends for many years.

"For what it's worth," Seth said, "I am sorry things ended like this." He took the cell phone from Ryan and then closed the morgue cooler door, leaving Ryan inside.

Thirty-Seven

Toni was busy getting Emily's schedule confirmed for the next couple of days when Sheriff McNeil called.

"Law office of Emily Bridges. How can I help you?" answered Toni cheerfully.

"Good afternoon, Toni. I was hoping your boss had some free time this afternoon," Mac quickly responded. He could hear Toni riffling through papers as she spoke on the phone.

"Hang on a sec, and I'll ask her. I think she was planning to stay late tonight to get caught up on a few things."

Without waiting for the sheriff's response, Toni put him on hold and quickly walked to Emily's office, poking her head inside the door. "Emily, the sheriff is on hold. He wants to know if you have any free time this afternoon."

Puzzled, Emily asked, "Did he say what he wanted?"

"Uh, no, he just asked if you were free. I told him you might be staying late tonight."

"Great, thanks," Emily muttered. "He is literally the last person I would want to see tonight—or any night, for that matter!"

Toni gave her a quick, apologetic frown and asked, "Do you want me to tell him you have plans? I don't mind. I am really sorry I told him you were going to stay late. I can tell him you changed your plans."

"No, it's OK, probably best to get this over with anyway. Something about him . . . I don't know. I don't get a warm, fuzzy feeling from him. But then again, he is a cop. You've known him a while, right?"

Laughing at her, Toni replied, "Oh, yeah, a soft, warm, fuzzy teddy bear! That one is not! I don't think I have ever seen him outside of work. In fact, I don't recall ever seeing him smile!" Toni turned to go to her desk, calling back to Emily, "I will patch him through to you."

Picking up the phone, she said, "Sheriff, I am patching you through to Emily." She could hear the irritation in Emily's voice as she picked up the call just before Toni hung up.

Emily didn't try to hide her dislike of the sheriff. "Sheriff, what I can do for you?" she asked dryly.

"Counselor, we had a few new developments in the detective's death. I was wondering if I could either meet with you after hours at your office or at my office. I know it's getting late in the day, but this is too important to wait." Mac waited for her to respond. He knew she would not readily agree to meeting at the station, and she probably wouldn't want to meet him alone in her office either. Just as he expected, she offered an alternative.

"Uh, Sheriff, I am going to be busy tonight at the office, but I could meet you for coffee afterward if that works for you. I should be done by eight or so." Emily was quietly praying he would forgo the meeting. To her dismay, he took her up on her offer.

"Sure, Counselor. Most places close early around here on a

weeknight, but I know of a small family café not too far away where we could have a coffee, maybe dinner if you're hungry."

"Sure, OK, sounds good. Just text me the address and I will be there," Emily stammered.

This was one dinner she wasn't looking forward to having. She glanced at Toni, who was packing up her things and getting ready to go home. She envied her; she seemed to be happy most days, and she had a supportive, loving family. The last thing Emily wanted was for Toni to think she was upset that she had told the sheriff she was going to be working late. "Toni," she called out.

Toni turned around at the desk and shouted back to her, "I am still here! I wouldn't leave without saying goodbye." She walked back over to Emily's office.

"I just wanted to thank you for all you have been doing for me. I know I am not always the easiest person to work with, and I didn't want you to think I was upset over the sheriff."

"No worries. I know him well enough to know it's best to just get the meeting with him over with. I have to pick up my daughter, so I will see you tomorrow morning!" Toni waited for Emily to say something, and for a brief moment, she thought she saw her eyes tear up.

Clearing her throat, Emily nodded her head, saying, "Yes, go get your daughter, and thanks again! I will see you in the morning!"

Emily finished up her last case, turned off the lights, locked up the office, and checked her text messages. Sure enough, there was an address for her to meet the sheriff. Reluctantly, she got into her car and programmed the navigator with the address. It wasn't one she recognized, and as dark as it was outside, she was hoping the street was well lit.

According to her navigator, the café was only about twelve miles from her office. It was overcast, and given it was late fall, it was already very dark. The navigator told her to take a left turn off the main road, which soon narrowed to a dirt-and-gravel road.

She hadn't gone far when she started thinking maybe she had programmed the navigator incorrectly or maybe the address was wrong. Then again, it wouldn't be the first time her navigator had sent her the wrong way. She laughed at herself as she recalled the time she and Eric had been trying to find a pizza place, and the navigator had taken them to an empty parking lot in the middle of nowhere! "Well, let's see where you are taking me. I can always turn the car around and tell the good sheriff I couldn't find his café," she said aloud to herself.

There didn't seem to be any good areas to make a quick U-turn, but just as she was thinking of making her own path back toward the main road, the navigator told her to make a right turn on to County Road 205 and her destination was a hundred meters from the turn. She slowed for the turn and noticed there was no signage for the café. "Yep, wrong address," she muttered. "I bet he won't believe I even tried to meet him."

She made the turn onto the narrow dirt road and stopped. The road was littered with large potholes. "Damn, this is not the right place!" she complained out loud. She put the car into reverse and set to back out when she noticed her rear lights were out and her backup camera wasn't working. Slamming her hands on the steering wheel in frustration, she knew she had no other option but to pull forward into this narrow road and find a way to turn the car around. She slowly crept forward, trying to avoid the deep holes in the road.

She had driven roughly fifty meters when her headlights lit up a building or house at the end of the road. It was no more than an old shack. "Yeah, some café!" she muttered. This dump was definitely not a café! It was the remnants of a small, old house. The windows were broken, and tattered curtains blew in the wind from around the window frames. The shack didn't look like it had ever been painted; it just had old wooden planks for the walls.

She cautiously continued the drive toward the shack and noticed something moving around the building. "Chickens!" she exclaimed. "How the hell did chickens get here? OK, just turn this car around and get the hell out of here!" she anxiously whispered to herself. She pulled up to the front of the shack, her headlights illuminating the way. In order to make the tight U-turn, she had to stop and back up a couple times, but she finally did it. Sighing in relief, she straightened her tires for the bumpy trip back down the road.

Blinding lights suddenly startled her, and she slammed on the brakes. Squinting, she tried to see who or what was blocking her path. When she heard a tap on her car window, she jumped in fear and surprise. Her heart was racing and pulsating loudly in her ears.

"Counselor!" she heard someone shout. For a brief moment she froze. "Emily, roll down the window!"

Stunned, she realized the sheriff was the one rapping on her window and scaring the hell out of her.

"Sheriff, you damn well better have a good reason for this!" Emily yelled at him as she rolled the window down.

Mac stepped back from her door and apologized. "Hey, I really am sorry. When you didn't show up at the café, I checked the text and realized my phone sent you the wrong address. I was driving and text-talking into the phone. Anyway, the translation was the wrong address. I knew this place and didn't want you to get stuck, so I came out here to find you. Again, I am real sorry." Mac smiled as he explained the mistake.

Emily was still unnerved, and his smile was causing her even more concern. What was it Toni had said about him? She couldn't shake the feeling that something wasn't right. "That's OK, Sheriff," she said carefully. "Can this wait until tomorrow afternoon? I just want to go home. Please move your car so I can get out," she hesitantly requested.

"Of course, Emily," he responded.

She didn't see him walk away. She did notice his headlights dimming but not turning off. She felt herself turning slowly from scared to angry. Taking her foot off the brake, she inched her car forward. Surely he would back up and let her out; maybe he thought he was helping her by lighting up the road. She felt a sudden, strong jolt as her right front tire hit a pothole and her seat belt tightened its grip. The tires spun, but the car didn't move forward. "Fuck!" she yelled as she struggled to release the seat belt and open the car door. She practically fell out of the car and was barely standing when she felt a sharp pain behind her temple. Instantly she crumpled to the ground.

Seth carried her limp body into the shanty. It was once an in-home pet parlor, complete with built-in tubs for washing the largest of dogs. But today it was simply a shack. He placed Emily into a solid wood chair, handcuffing her wrists to the back rail of the chair. Using zip ties and duct tape, he secured her ankles and calves to the legs of the chair, and lastly, he removed her shoes. Satisfied that she was going nowhere and could not get herself loose, he threw cold water on her face. Dazed, she lifted her head and looked around the dark room, her eyes finally settling on him. She tried to move but quickly came to the realization she wasn't able to. Scrambling for words, she weakly asked, "Sheriff? What's going on? Where am I? Who is here? Sheriff, is that you?"

Seth stood in the shadows of the room watching her, waiting, but not speaking. There was no reason to gag her; she could yell and scream all she wanted. There was no one, no building, no businesses, no homes for miles, and no one was going to hear her. All that was around the shanty was swampland. When he was certain she could not escape, he quietly stepped out of the room onto the broken-down front porch of the shanty. He had one more person to see tonight.

Thirty-Eight

"Eric, Sheriff McNeil returning your call."

Before Mac could finish, Eric interrupted him. "Yes! Sheriff, hello! Thanks for returning my call. I still can't reach Brad. It's been over twenty-four hours! I think we need to be looking for him."

It was late Monday night. The funerals for Brad's family had been the day before, and the fire at the airport was the night of the funerals. Eric hadn't spoken to Brad since the funerals.

Stammering, he continued, "Uh, look, Sheriff, I think something happened to him." He was taking a chance calling the police, but he needed to know if Brad was dead or if he was on the run, and he wasn't about to risk exposing himself with the monsignor. There were only a few places Brad could run, and he knew all of them. He had scheduled his flight to Denmark the following morning. Everything was in place for the final charter, and unless he found his partner, he wasn't going to have a copilot. But either way, he was going to be on that plane. He would deal with Brad later. For now, he needed to play the part of a worried business partner.

Mac listened and heard panic or maybe nervousness in Eric's voice. "I'm glad you called me back. I needed to talk to you about your business partner, Dr. Rivers. Are you still in town?"

Eric hadn't yet left for Boston and was sitting in the office he shared with Brad. He really didn't want to meet the sheriff at the airstrip. The last thing he needed was for the sheriff to stumble across the flight schedules. "I can meet you anywhere you pick, Sheriff," he answered carefully. "I am actually heading back to Boston. I have a flight to catch in the morning. I can meet you tonight if it's quick. Do you want me to go the police station?"

"No, let's meet at Emily Bridges's office. You know her? The attorney?" Mac wondered what Eric was going to say, if he would admit to knowing her.

"Uh, yeah, sure I know who she is. We can meet there if she is still in her office. It's rather late." Eric was scrambling, trying to figure out why the sheriff would want to meet after hours in Emily's office. "Sheriff, can I ask what this is about?"

Instead of answering Eric's question, Mac replied, "I'll meet you there around eight thirty. Let me know if you are going to be late." He didn't give Eric time to object, instead disconnecting the call.

The sheriff was already waiting for Eric in the alley adjacent to Emily's building. The parking lot was dark except for one street light in the middle of the lot. Emily's office lights were on, not because she was working late but because the cleaning crew was there. Just a few minutes after 8:30 p.m., Eric pulled his black BMW, with its headlights off, into the parking lot and parked close to the building's entrance.

"Emily, answer the damn phone," Eric loudly complained. Why wasn't she answering the phone? He wasn't about to go inside her office until she answered him, and he wasn't about to be ambushed by some pushy small-town cop!

Mac was walking toward the entrance of the building when Eric got out of his car. He quickly called out, "Mr. Wilkerson, I need you to come with me."

Eric looked up at the sheriff in surprise. "Sure, whatever you need, Sheriff. I thought we were meeting in Emily's office." Eric hadn't noticed any cars when he pulled into the parking lot. "I don't see your car. Where are you parked, Sheriff?" Eric glanced around the parking lot and realized there were no cars in the lot, not even Emily's.

Mac gestured toward the alley. "I had a call about a prowler in back of the building. Was just walking around to the front when you pulled in."

Nodding his head, Eric asked, "Did you find anyone?"

"Nope, no one there. You can leave your car here. I'll bring you back afterward," Mac assured him. "Emily called and canceled on us." Waving at the building, Mac continued, "It's just the cleaning crew up there."

Eric gave the parking lot one last quick glance before walking with Mac toward the police cruiser. When they reached the car, Mac opened the passenger door and motioned for Eric to get in. "Hmmm, really, Sheriff? You want me to sit in the back of the car?"

"Yeah, I still have the waders from last night in the front seat, plus the laptop that is usually connected to the dash—damn thing fell off. It's on the seat. No room for you up front." Mac stepped back, giving him more room to get into the car.

"Sheriff, where are we going? I think you just passed the police department," Eric cautiously said.

Sheriff McNeil didn't answer. He may have been driving in silence, but he was fully aware of his passenger, and he was enjoying watching Eric Wilkerson grow increasingly nervous and frightened.

Thirty-Nine

He was surprised his passenger kept quiet for most of the drive. He noticed Eric trying to open the car doors and windows. His movements were slow and well thought out, but it wouldn't matter. Eric was only getting out of the cruiser when Seth wanted him out.

"Sheriff, look, I am not sure what your plans are, but you need to understand I am an attorney, and this is false imprisonment! I will sue you and the county."

"Counselor, do you expect to survive the night?" Seth looked at him in the rearview mirror.

Eric was struggling to control his growing apprehension, but he also knew everyone had a price, and he just needed to find the sheriff's price. "Sheriff, I can pay you whatever you want. Just forget what I said about suing you and the county." Not getting a reply, he pleaded, "Come on, this isn't funny anymore. What do you want from me?"

The cruiser took a sharp turn onto what Eric felt was probably a dirt or stone road. He could feel the loose gravel under the car's tires, and almost immediately after turning, the lights of the distant city were gone. Except for the gleam of the headlights, it was pitch black. The cruiser stopped in front of what looked like an old house or shack.

Sheriff McNeil turned off the engine. Turning to Eric, he said, "You ready to meet with Emily?" Hearing Eric inhale sharply gave him a moment of satisfaction. He almost wished he could take a picture of the surprise and shock on Eric's face as he slowly began to understand that Emily hadn't canceled; she was inside.

"Emily is in there?" Eric slowly asked. "Why would she be in there?"

"Eric, I am going to open the car door. But before I do, we need to reach an understanding. I want you to look at me and listen carefully. Are you ready to do that?" Seth had turned sideways in the front seat to look at Eric. "I said look at me. I won't repeat myself, Eric."

Stammering, Eric answered him. "Uh, yeah, yes! I understand you."

"Good. As I said, I am going to open the car door. You are going to exit the car and stand next to the car until I tell you to move. When I tell you to move, you will slowly walk toward the front porch of the house in front of this car. You will not make any attempt to run or fight me." Holding up what looked like a square remote control, Seth continued talking. "You are going to do exactly what you are told to do, or I will activate this remote. This remote will send a signal to a chair that Emily is sitting on. The remote will signal a bomb that is under her chair to explode. She will either die instantly or the bomb will blow her in half and she will bleed out. Do you understand?" Seth waited for a response from Eric.

Eric looked evenly at Seth. He was no longer fearful of the sheriff. Now he was angry. "Yes, Sheriff, I understand." He had every intention of figuring a way out of this.

The sheriff opened the car door, and Eric carefully got out of the cruiser. Once he was standing by the car door, he felt a sharp pain in his left flank as he was jabbed with a nightstick.

"Walk," instructed Seth.

"It's dark," complained Eric. "I can barely see where I am going! Do you have a light or something?"

"Barely seeing is better than seeing nothing." Seth pushed him toward the steps. "So get walking."

Eric stumbled up the steps and then into the front door of the house. He thought he could hear breathing. *Thank God*, he thought. *Emily is still alive.* "Emily," he whispered.

Seth flipped a switch by the door, instantly illuminating the room. Looking across the room, Eric gasped as he saw Emily sitting in a chair, her arms behind her back. She was secured to the wooden chair with what looked like ropes and duct tape. But he could see that she was breathing! He slowly exhaled as he realized she was alive but that neither of them was going to stay alive if he didn't do something. She slowly raised her head, squinting her eyes as they adjusted to the light.

"Over here," Seth said. Eric struggled to take his eyes off Emily because he knew he had to pay attention to the sheriff. He turned slowly toward him and saw that the remote had been replaced with a semiautomatic aimed at his head. Using the gun, Seth pointed to a metal folding chair that was sitting in what looked like a tub. "Go sit down on that chair," Seth instructed.

Eric shook his head no. "Sheriff, I am not sure what is going on here, but you need to let us go. Whatever is wrong, we can fix." Eric knew if he stepped away from Emily, she didn't have a chance.

"Eric," Emily managed to say. Her voice was hoarse and dry, but she was speaking. "He's not the sheriff."

"I am the sheriff, Emily. You know that. Just ask your paralegal." Seth motioned for Eric to sit down.

"OK, OK, I am doing what you want. Can you at least tell us why you are doing this?" Eric climbed into the tub and sat gingerly on the metal seat.

"Of course I will explain why you both are here. But before we get started, you need to put these on." Seth tossed Eric a pair of handcuffs.

"You can't be serious! You already have us at your mercy! I am not putting these on!" Eric shouted back at Seth.

"Eric, do you remember what I told you Emily was sitting on?"

"What am I sitting on?" Emily shouted back, instantly panicking. "Eric!" she shouted again. "What am I sitting on?"

"OK, I am putting on the handcuffs! See? They're on! Now tell us what the fuck we are doing here. What the hell is going on?" Eric struggled to keep his composure. He knew a killer when he saw one. Brad was the coldest person he had ever known, but this guy, whoever he was, made Brad look like a nice guy. He had no doubt the sheriff had killed Brad. Seth stood between Eric and Emily, and he was watching them both, but the gun was pointed at Eric. His voice quivering, Eric asked again, but this time he lowered his voice. "Listen, we did what you asked. We aren't giving you any trouble. Hell, we won't even say anything, Sheriff. Just let us go. No reason to even tell us why we are here."

Ignoring Eric's pleas, Seth turned his attention to Emily. "You asked what you were sitting on. Do you still want to know?" He didn't wait for Emily to answer. "Tell me about your friend Rachel."

Emily gave him a stunned look. "Rachel? I don't understand," she stammered.

Nodding his head, Seth replied, "Your friend, Rachel. You remember her. You allowed her husband to kill her and get away with it. You profited from her death. Are you starting to understand?" Seth's voice was getting louder with each word as he allowed his anger and pain to rise. "How much did Brad and Eric pay you to ignore the FAA report and not file charges?"

Emily struggled to break loose from the chair. She had no intention of answering this lunatic. "What am I sitting on?" she yelled at him. "You tell me now, Sheriff! What am I sitting on?"

"A chair. You are sitting on a chair. I am not going to waste time with you. I asked you a question. You accepted half a million in exchange for Rachel's life! How much would you spend to save your life? How much, Counselor? How much is your pathetic life worth?"

Emily stammered to answer him. "I am sorry. Stephanie was still alive. She had already lost so much. Putting Brad, her dad, in prison for what could have been an accident would have only made her lose more. I couldn't do that to her." Emily was now pleading with him. "Sheriff, you must know there was no clear evidence the accident was intentional!"

"Maybe not, but that doesn't explain the painting you took to cover it up, does it?" Seth asked her.

"What painting?" Emily cried out.

"Did you think it would go unnoticed? Granted, it's been seventy years since it was lost, but that painting in your conference room isn't a print."

Emily sank back in the chair. She no longer looked scared; instead, she looked defiant. Leveling her eyes at him, she took in a deep breath and said, "What difference would it have made, Sheriff? They weren't coming back."

"Rachel's death wasn't the only time you accepted money to hide the truth, was it, Counselor?" He waited for her to show some sign of acknowledgment. When she didn't answer, he told her. "James—do you remember him?"

Glaring at him, Emily ignored the question, screaming instead, "Why do you care? Who was Rachel to you anyway? James was a long time ago! Are you some sick type of vigilante?" Following her outburst, she inhaled deeply. The man she thought was the sheriff wasn't looking at her or Eric. He was staring at the floor. If she was going to die, she was going to die fighting, not sitting in a chair silently.

Seth inhaled deeply. He had planned for this day for a long time, and now that it was finally here, he was finding it difficult to speak. Struggling with the words, he said, "I'm much more than just Sheriff

McNeil. My name is Seth Richards. Your friend Rachel was the mother of my daughters, Stephanie and Elizabeth."

Seth waited for both of them to react. Sensing their shock, he continued, "Rachel and I were childhood sweethearts and lovers after college. There is no reason to go into why she stayed married to Dr. Rivers. All you need to know is I am not a vigilante."

Seth paused and then angrily began shouting, his voice becoming louder with each word. "What I am is angry and pissed off, most importantly at you, Emily"—he pointed at her as he screamed—"because you failed to bring Rachel's killer to justice and have shown over the past several years that you will never choose justice over money, fame, or your career. And since you won't, I will." He lowered his voice. "Neither one of you will leave here alive. No one is coming to rescue you."

"Why Detective Connard?" Emily shouted at him. "I get why you cared about Rachel and even Stephanie and Elizabeth, although you obviously didn't care enough to be a part of their lives before they died!"

Seth laughed. "Why Connard? Because I felt like it, and it was easy. In a nutshell, that was the reason. Counselor, you aren't as observant as you think you are. Before I became the sheriff here, I worked with Connard. I was one of the hundreds of detectives in Boston. The fat fuck actually thought I was going to hire him. You did, however, accidentally stumble across him on the beach. That was perfect. I couldn't have planned that one better."

"I knew you?" Emily stammered.

"The evidence you suppressed that would have exonerated James was collected by me," he said.

Finally, a look of understanding or recognition came over Emily's face.

"Sheriff, or Seth, listen to me," said Eric. You said yourself that Rachel was friends with Emily. You claim you loved her and that you are doing this out of some type of obligation you feel." Eric believed he had one shot to save them. He had to reason with this guy.

Otherwise, they would both be killed. "Come on, Sheriff. If you knew Rachel, you would know she wouldn't want this. She wouldn't want Emily to suffer."

"You are right about one thing, Eric. Rachel wouldn't want Emily to suffer."

Emily exhaled in relief. The early-morning light was seeping through the cracks of the windows, and for the first time since she'd left her office the evening before, she felt as if she would survive and have one hell of a story to tell. She turned to look at Eric just as she saw Seth level the gun toward her and heard Eric stammer.

Before she could react, Seth pulled the trigger, killing her instantly. Turning to Eric, he said, "She didn't suffer."

The sound was deafening. Eric was shocked at how loud the shot was. He couldn't breathe. Emily was slumped forward in the chair. Blood oozed from her forehead and ran down her face, dripping onto the floor next to her chair. Yelling, he finally looked away from her. "You sick fuck! Do you really think this is going to change anything?"

Seth shook his head at Eric. "You still don't get it, do you? This isn't about changing anything. This is about retribution." With each additional word, Seth raised his voice. "This has never been about change! I don't have time to play with you anymore, Eric. I have a flight to catch and a monsignor to meet."

"He will kill you!" Eric shouted. "Wait, what you are doing?"

Seth walked to the back of the tub. "You noticed you are sitting on a metal chair in a groomer's bathtub? You see, Brad died in a fire, just like Rachel and the children. You are going to die in this tub." Seth turned the water on and watched as the tub began to fill. Taking a thick, black electrical cord from the fuse box, he placed it in the tub.

In his attempted to get up, Eric fell on his side, still strapped to the metal chair. "You're crazy!" he screamed at Seth. "You won't get away with this!"

"You're going to want to watch this," Seth jokingly said to Eric as he plugged the cord into the outlet. Eric screamed as the cord became a live wire and the water trickling into the tub became the current of electricity. Just before Eric stopped screaming, Seth doused the old shanty with gas and watched it burn. When he was satisfied that Eric was dead, he got back into the cruiser and left for the airport. He had a flight to catch.

Fourty

He barely made his flight. He was pleasantly surprised at how easy it was to get through airport security. Then again, it was a nonstop international flight out of Boston to Copenhagen. Once he was on the plane, he settled back in his seat and allowed himself to relax. He was exhausted. For the first time in days, sleep came easy.

"Put your tray tables in the upright position, and secure all personal belongings under the seat. Please make sure your seat belts are fastened." He woke up to the automatic announcement. The flight was about to land. Looking out the window, he felt calm, almost satisfied.

It was late fall, and northern Europe was more than chilly. It was downright freezing! His last conversation with Monsignor Tedesco had been just a few hours before takeoff. His flight had been delayed a bit. If he missed the deadline, not only would he fail in bringing final retribution to those who needed it the most, but people who had suffered years ago—other innocents who had died and lost everything, whose families were still waiting to get back their loved one's property—would continue to suffer. This last kill was more than getting vengeance; it was about making things right. He was the only one who could make it right. Failing wasn't an option.

"Flight delayed due to air traffic congestion, just landed" was the text message he fired off to Tedesco once the plane landed.

"Meet at hangar B12," responded Tedesco via text.

The VS nerve gas was placed inside tiny breakaway pill containers. Each "pill" had been molded into an oblong tablet, and to ensure they didn't accidentally break, they were placed securely in a pill box, which was placed in a plastic container. For the final part of his plan to work, the monsignor and his bodyguards would have to get close enough for him to break open the pill container and crush the tablet so he could gently toss it in the air toward his intended target. Only a small amount was needed to elicit the desired and almost immediate response: death. He had enough antidote in his pocket in case he accidently poisoned himself. Not that he would mind; if he died finishing this mission, he knew he would die successful. He couldn't die without ensuring the monsignor was dead along with his remaining partners.

The private hangars were not too far from where his flight landed. He quickly made his way out of baggage claim and briskly walked to B12.

"Dr. Rivers? Is that you or Eric?" Monsignor Tedesco shouted at Seth as he was walking toward the hangar.

Seth didn't answer, instead raising his hand over his head as if to signal the monsignor. Seth knew how Dr. Rivers dressed, and he'd made certain he was dressed much like the doctor. He was wearing suit pants, a sweater, a blazer, and a black leather hip-length jacket with a scarf around his neck and lower face. Just like Eric wore when he flew, Seth was wearing a Boston Red Sox baseball cap.

Before he could reach the hangar, Liam hollered for him to stop. "That will be close enough," Liam said as he carefully walked toward Seth, followed closely by another man.

Seth slowly raised his hand to the scarf and carefully positioned it over his nose and mouth. Under the scarf was a N95 one-way mask. Once the two men were a couple of feet away from Seth, he removed his left hand from his pocket, and in what appeared to be the initiation of a handshake, released the VS nerve gas. Liam and his partner stopped almost instantly. Both men grabbed at their throats. Foam began to bubble at their mouths, and blood dripped from their eyes and nose, and before the monsignor could see what was happening, the men fell to the ground. Seth stepped over the convulsing men and walked slowly and purposefully toward Monsignor Tedesco.

"Stop!" ordered the monsignor. "Don't come any closer."

Seth continued to walk toward him without answering.

"Did you hear me? I said to stop!"

"Monsignor Tedesco? I assume that is your name." Seth finally stopped, but not before ensuring he was within range of releasing the gas.

"You are not Dr. Rivers or Eric Wilkerson! Who are you? If you are here to try to bargain for more money, you will be disappointed. I am not prepared to part with any additional funds," Tedesco firmly stated. He was not afraid of this American. He seriously doubted he would harm him, as his position with the Vatican made him a powerful adversary. "Perhaps I need to inform you of who I am?" Tedesco said while taking a step backward.

"I know who you are, I know what you are, and, most importantly, I know what you are doing and what you have been doing. Do you really think that after all of this comes out, anyone will care who or what position you held? Other than the fact that you used that position to profit from the suffering, torture, and deaths of millions?" Seth moved slightly closer to Tedesco.

Tedesco asked him a second time, "Who are you?" This time his voice was shaky.

"Who I am doesn't really matter," Seth managed to answer before Tedesco interrupted him with another question.

"What do you want? Name your price! Everyone has a price! Including a nut job like you!" Tedesco nervously shouted. The hangar was empty, but Tedesco was hoping someone would hear them. He stole a quick look around the area and, seeing no one, took another step back.

"My price is your death. It's very simply, really. My price from you is the same price all the donors of your precious thievery paid. My price won't reimburse any of them, but it will ensure that you and your partners no longer profit from the millions of dollars' worth of stolen art, gold, and other artifacts and valuables that need to be returned to their rightful countries and families," Seth said with a tight smile. "My price ensures the return of millions. Are you prepared to meet my price?" He very slowly began walking toward Tedesco. "Any last words, or perhaps a final prayer to your savior, Monsignor?"

Tedesco finally realized he was going to die. He didn't take Seth up on his offer of a final prayer or a final word. Instead he turned and tried to run. Seth was faster and stronger. He quickly caught the monsignor, and placing his hand over the other man's mouth, he released the final dose of VS nerve gas.

Seth's mask was still in place. He was protected. He waited and watched Monsignor Tedesco die. He had successfully made his final kill.

Fourty-One

The old house glistened in the moonlight. He knew this would be the last time he saw the house, the last time he could see where he had first met Rachel. He was no longer angry. The sadness and pain were gone. What was left was a feeling of emptiness.

He had taken the photo from his foyer table with him when he kidnapped Emily and Eric. He kept it with him on the flights to and back from Copenhagen. Taking it from his pocket now, he looked at the two of them as children. After Rachel had died, this photo kept him alive and gave him purpose, and he dreaded the time when that purpose no longer existed. He had often wondered what he would feel once the pain and anger of his loss were gone. It surprised him that not only did he feel empty, he also felt a sense of freedom.

"I had a feeling I would see you again," Seth lightly laughed as he turned to greet his old friend.

Ryan stood in the street in front of Seth's childhood home. "Mac, or Seth, I'm not sure what to call you."

"Call me whatever name you like. I'll answer you." Seth had been standing on the front steps when Ryan came out of the shadows. "What are you doing here, Ryan?"

"Well, Mac, it's an interesting story. I did some of my own investigative work and found out who you are and where you used to live." Ryan kept his hands in the pockets of his jacket. He didn't think he would need it, but he had a snub-nosed .38-caliber revolver tightly gripped in his right hand.

"And what did you learn?" Seth asked.

"You were not easy to find, my friend. I only found you through Rachel."

Seth nodded. "Yes, I imagine that's about the only way you or anyone could find me."

"I have a lot of questions, and I have a feeling you aren't going to answer any of them. But I am going to ask anyway."

Seth nodded. "I will answer you. But I have a question first. Then I will answer yours."

"Go ahead, ask."

"How long do we have, Ryan? Did you notify the authorities that I'm here?"

Shaking his head, Ryan said, "No, no, I didn't. I may still do that. I haven't decided. But I haven't yet."

"What are your questions?" Seth asked.

"I went through the history of this town. Your family owned quite a bit of this place." Ryan nodded toward the old factory and house. "I noticed you still own all of this. Why have you kept these properties?"

"Isn't it obvious? You said you researched the history of the town. If you did your research, you should know that selling this place isn't in my best interest." Seth took a step closer to Ryan.

"The missing children occurred when you were just a boy

yourself. Are you telling me you had something to do with their disappearances?" Ryan slowly asked.

Seth glanced down the street before answering. "Ryan, all I am going to acknowledge is that I learned at a young age that I had a talent and a hobby. I made a promise many years ago to ignore that part of myself, and I kept that promise until Stephanie died."

"How many people have you killed, Mac?" Ryan asked.

"I think you have a pretty good idea how many, Ryan. Let me put your mind at ease. After I made my promise, I only killed people who needed to be killed and in a manner I felt was necessary. Dr. Rivers killed eight people, and of the eight he killed, six were children. Stephanie and Elizabeth were my daughters! I would have kept my promise to Rachel, all those years ago, to not kill again, but after Stephanie's death, all that changed. Are you really going to stand there and pretend he was justified and I am not?" Seth felt the anger he thought was gone rising as his voice became louder.

Ryan looked closely at Seth, and for a moment he saw his former friend in the other man's eyes. Instead of being afraid of him or seeing him as a crazy killer, he began to feel a deep sorrow for him. "Mac, listen, I am sorry all of that happened. I agree, he murdered both of his families. I also know how horrible a death they each had. I can't imagine how any of them felt, and I certainly can't imagine the pain they suffered. I also know you spared me for some reason, and I don't know why."

"I already told you, Ryan, I wasn't going to kill a good man."

Ryan nodded his head in understanding. "One last question. Were you involved in the death of the priest in Copenhagen and the death of this partners? It's all over the news that they were smuggling art and gold out of various places in Europe, and it's speculated that Dr. Rivers and Eric Wilkerson were their pilots and partners. We both know each are dead, although Eric's body hasn't been found yet. In case you didn't know, Emily Bridges is missing too. Her paralegal reported her missing yesterday."

Seth didn't answer. Instead, he waited for Ryan to make the connection.

"Mac, I made my decision. I am going to make a call. I have no choice. However, I do have a choice as to when I make that call. You're going to leave. I don't care where you go. I don't care what you do. But you are leaving. If I have the slightest hint that you are killing, regardless of your rationale, I will go after you myself."

Ryan turned and started walking away from Seth, wondering if he would make it to his car alive. When he got to his car, he unlocked the front door and turned to look back at the house and at Seth. The front of the house was empty. No one stood on the steps, and the front doors remained closed. Ryan looked up and down the street but didn't see Seth. He got into his car and let the engine idle for a few minutes.

He wasn't sure if his decision was the right one or not, but he knew that no one Seth had killed had been worthy of saving. He would keep his promise. He would watch and wait.

Acknowledgment

I want to thank Dr. C. Moma for his review and critique of *Retribution.* You inspired me to finish this project! Thank you so much!

Made in the USA
Columbia, SC
09 July 2020

13557943R00136